seeds of change

also edited by
john joseph adams

WASTELANDS:
STORIES OF THE APOCALYPSE

THE LIVING DEAD

seeds of change

edited by
john joseph adams

PRIME BOOKS

SEEDS OF CHANGE

Compilation and introduction © 2008 John Joseph Adams

"N-Words" © 2008 Ted Kosmatka
"The Future by Degrees" © 2008 Joseph E. Lake, Jr.
"Drinking Problem" © 2008 K. D. Wentworth
"Endosymbiont" © 2008 Blake Charlton
"A Dance Called Armageddon" © 2008 Ken MacLeod
"Arties Aren't Stupid" © 2008 Jeremiah Tolbert
"Faceless in Gethsemane" © 2008 Mark Budz
"Spider the Artist" © 2008 Nnedi Okorafor-Mbachu
"Resistance" © 2008 Tobias S. Buckell

Earth graphic by Beboy

PRIME BOOKS
www.prime-books.com

No portion of this book may be reproduced by any means, mechanical, electronic, or otherwise, without first obtaining the permission of the copyright holder, except in the case of brief quotations embodied in critical articles or reviews. For more information, contact Prime Books at prime@prime-books.com.

ISBN: 978-0-8095-7310-3

acknowledgments

Many thanks to the following:

Sean Wallace of Prime Books, who not only gave me the opportunity to edit my first original anthology, but saved me the hassle of having to pitch it to him.

Also at Prime: Stephen Segal, who offered up the initial concept for the book and did all the design work that made the finished product look so pretty.

If I were Spider-Man, Gordon Van Gelder would be the radioactive spider that imbued me with my superpowers. Okay, that might be overstating the case a bit, but before I went to work for him, I was just your average SF-writer geek, and now I've got books with my name on them.

Beth Wodzinski, and the other folks behind *Shimmer Magazine*, who perhaps helped pave my road to editing original anthologies by showcasing my talents as the guest editor of their bloodthirsty pirate issue.

Jenny Rappaport, agent extraordinaire, for selling that first anthology, and for helping me keep the ball rolling. Also, for dog-sitting.

Jack Kincaid, for his friendship and for his feedback, and also for putting together that frickin' sweet book trailer for the anthology.

The NYC Geek Posse—consisting of Christopher M. Cevasco, Douglas E. Cohen, David Barr Kirtley, Andrea

Kail, and Rob Bland, among others (i.e., the NYCGP Auxiliary)—for giving me an excuse to come out of my editorial cave once in a while.

Contributors Jeremiah Tolbert and Blake Charlton, both of whom provided some tremendously useful feedback on a variety of anthology-related topics, and, of course, for writing me such awesome stories.

And thanks, too, to the rest of the writers who appear in this book—you guys made my job pretty easy.

contents

introduction *John Joseph Adams*	9
n-words *Ted Kosmatka*	13
the future by degrees *Jay Lake*	37
drinking problem *K.D. Wentworth*	57
endosymbiont *Blake Charlton*	83
a dance called armageddon *Ken MacLeod*	133
arties aren't stupid *Jeremiah Tolbert*	145
faceless in gethsemane *Mark Budz*	165
spider the artist *Nnedi Okorafor-Mbachu*	193
resistance *Tobias S. Buckell*	217

introduction
John Joseph Adams

Ursula K. Le Guin once wrote, "Science fiction is not predictive; it is descriptive"—which is to say that it uses the future as a lens to examine the here and now. Sometimes the paradigms of the present must be challenged, and one of the ways to do that is through science fiction.

I asked the contributors to this anthology to write about paradigm shifts—technological, scientific, political, or cultural—and how individuals and societies deal with such changes. The idea is to challenge our current paradigms and speculate on how they might evolve in the future, either for better or for worse.

seeds of change

Several of the stories approach the theme directly with current, topical issues—Ted Kosmatka tackles racism; Tobias S. Buckell explores the importance of voting; K. D. Wentworth takes a humorous look at a possible recycling revolution; Jay Lake ponders a world-changing technological advance and the market forces conspiring against it; Nnedi Okorafor-Mbachu takes us to the Niger Delta, where oil is a top commodity and people a secondary consideration.

After selecting the table of contents, I asked the contributors to describe how they interpreted the theme. Responses were thoughtful and diverse, but perhaps Blake Charlton captured the essence of the anthology best: "Fiction can be a mode of social change," he said. "The most important revolutions begin quietly; the perception of injustice and suffering must precede any action against them."

It is my hope that reading these stories inspires some to plant their own seeds of change—that when we see something wrong, we'll do something about it, whether that means writing to your representative in Congress or researching a cure for a disease or simply speaking out against inequality and prejudice. We're all in this together—and the first step toward change can begin with any one of us.

• • •

n-words

>>>

Ted Kosmatka is the author of about a dozen stories, which have sold to both literary journals and genre magazines such as Asimov's Science Fiction, The Magazine of Fantasy & Science Fiction, Cemetery Dance, *and* Ideomancer. *His story "Deadnauts" was nominated for a British Science Fiction Association Award, and his story "The Prophet of Flores" was reprinted in both Gardner Dozois's* The Year's Best Science Fiction *and Jonathan Strahan's* The Best Science Fiction and Fantasy of the Year.

As is probably evident from the title, "N-Words" is a story about racism. The subject has long been of scientific interest to Kosmatka; in college, he read every issue of a prominent scientific journal, dating back nearly 100 years, and it changed his whole view of science. "I learned that science is fallible," Kosmatka said, "and that in the wrong hands, it can absolutely be racist."

N-words

Ted Kosmatka

They came from test tubes. They came pale as ghosts with eyes as blue-white as glacier ice. They came first out of Korea.

I try to picture David's face in my head, but I can't. They've told me this is temporary—a kind of shock that happens sometimes when you've seen a person die that way. Although I try to picture David's face, it's only his pale eyes I can see.

N-words

My sister squeezes my hand in the back of the limo. "It's almost over," she says.

Up the road, against the long, wrought iron railing, the protestors grow excited as our procession approaches. They're standing in the snow on both sides of the cemetery gates, men and women wearing hats and gloves and looks of righteous indignation, carrying signs I refuse to read.

My sister squeezes my hand again. Before today I had not seen her in almost four years. But today she helped me pick out my black dress. She helped me with my stockings and my shoes. She helped me dress my son, who is not yet three, and who doesn't like ties—and who is now sleeping on the seat across from us without any understanding of what he's lost.

"Are you going to be okay?" my sister asks.

"No," I say. "I don't think I am."

The limo slows as it turns onto cemetery property, and the mob rushes in, shouting obscenities. Protestors push against the sides of the vehicle.

"You aren't wanted here!" someone shouts, and then an old man's face is against the glass, his eyes wild. "God's will be done!" he shrieks. "For the wages of sin is death."

The limo rocks under the press of the crowd, and the driver accelerates until we are past them, moving up the slope toward the other cars.

"What's wrong with them?" my sister whispers. "What kind of people would do that on a day like today?"

seeds of change

You'd be surprised, I think. *Maybe your neighbors. Maybe mine.* But I look out the window and say nothing. I've gotten used to saying nothing.

SHE'D SHOWN UP at my house this morning a little after 6:00. I'd opened the door, and she stood there in the cold, and neither of us spoke, neither of us sure what to say after so long.

"I heard about it on the news," she said finally. "I came on the next plane. I'm so sorry, Mandy."

There are things I wanted to say then—things that welled up inside of me like a bubble ready to burst, and I opened my mouth to scream at her, but what came out belonged to a different person: it came out a pathetic sob, and she stepped forward and wrapped her arms around me, my sister again after all these years.

The limo slows near the top of the hill, and the procession tightens. Headstones crowd the roadway. I see the tent up ahead, green; its canvas sides billow in and out with the wind, like a giant's breathing. Two-dozen gray folding chairs crouch in straight rows beneath it.

The limo stops.

"Should we wake the boy?" my sister asks.

"I don't know."

"Do you want me to carry him?"

"Can you?"

She looks at the child. "He's only three?"

"No," I say. "Not yet."

N-words

"He's big for his age. I mean, isn't he? I'm not around kids much."

"The doctors say he's big."

My sister leans forward and touches his milky white cheek. "He's beautiful," she says. I try not to hear the surprise in her voice. People are never aware of that tone when they use it, revealing what their expectations had been. But I'm past being offended by what people reveal unconsciously. Now it's only intent that offends. "He really is beautiful," she says again.

"He's his father's son," I say.

Ahead of us, people climb from their cars. The priest is walking toward the grave.

"It's time," my sister says. She opens the door and we step out into the cold.

THEY CAME FIRST out of Korea. But that's wrong, of course. History has an order to its telling. It would be more accurate to say it started in Britain. After all it was Harding who published first; it was Harding who shook the world with his announcement. And it was Harding who the religious groups burned in effigy on their church lawns.

Only later did the Koreans reveal they'd accomplished the same goal two years before, and the proof was already out of diapers. And it was only later, much later, that the world would recognize the scope of what they'd done.

When the Yeong Bae fell to the People's Party, the Korean labs were emptied, and there were suddenly *thou-*

seeds of change

sands of them—little blond and red-haired orphans, pale as ghosts, starving on the Korean streets as society crumbled around them. The ensuing wars and regime changes destroyed much of the supporting scientific data—but the children themselves, the ones who survived, were incontrovertible. There was no mistaking what they were.

It was never fully revealed why the Yeong Bae had developed the project in the first place. Perhaps they'd been after a better soldier. Or perhaps they'd done it for the oldest reason: because they could.

What is known for certain is that in 2001 disgraced stem cell biologist Hwang Woo-Suk cloned the world's first dog, an afghan. In 2006, he revealed that he'd tried and failed to clone a mammoth on three separate occasions. Western labs had talked about it, but the Koreans had actually tried. This would prove to be the pattern.

In 2011 the Koreans finally succeeded, and a mammoth was born from an elephant surrogate. Other labs followed. Other species. The Pallid Beach Mouse. The Pyrenean Ibex. And older things. Much older. The best scientists in the US had to leave the country to do their work. US laws against stem cell research didn't stop scientific advancement; it only stopped it from occurring in the US. Instead, Britain, China, and India won patents for the procedures. Cancers were cured. Most forms of blindness, MS, and Parkinson's. When Congress eventually legalized the medical procedures, but not the lines of research which lead to them, the hypocrisy was too much, and even the

N-words

most loyal American cyto-researchers left the country.

Harding was among this final wave, leaving the United States to set up a lab in the UK. In 2013, he was the first to bring back the Thylacine. In the winter of 2015, someone brought him a partial skull from a museum exhibit. The skull was doliocephalic—long, low, large. The bone was heavy, the cranial vault enormous—part of a skullcap that had been found in 1857 in a quarry in the Neander valley.

SNOW CRUNCHES UNDER our feet as my sister and I move outside the limo. The wind is freezing, and my legs grow numb in my thin slacks. It is fitting he is being buried on a day like today; David was never bothered by the cold.

My sister gestures toward the limo's open door. "Are you sure you want to bring the boy? I could stay with him in the car."

"He should be here," I say. "He should see it."

"He won't understand."

"No, but later he might remember he was here," I say. "Maybe that will matter."

"He's too young to remember."

"He remembers everything." I lean into the shadows and wake the boy. His eyes open like blue lights. "Come, Sean, it's time to wake up."

He rubs a pudgy fist into his eyes and says nothing. He is a quiet boy, my son. Out in the cold, I pull a hat down over his ears. The boy walks between my sister and me, holding our hands.

seeds of change

At the top of the hill, Dr. Michaels is there to greet us, along with other faculty from Stanford. They offer their condolences, and I work hard not to break down. Dr. Michaels looks like he hasn't slept. I introduce my sister and hands are shaken.

"You never mentioned you had a sister," he says.

I only nod. Dr. Michaels looks down at the boy and tugs the child's hat.

"Do you want me to pick you up?" he asks.

"Yeah." Sean's voice is small and scratchy from sleep. It is not an odd voice for a boy his age. It is a normal voice. Dr. Michaels lifts him, and the child's blue eyes close again.

We stand in silence in the cold. Mourners gather around the grave.

"I still can't believe it," Dr. Michaels says. He's swaying slightly, unconsciously rocking the boy. It is something only a man who has been a father would do, though his own children are grown.

"It's like I'm another person now," I say. "Only I haven't learned how to be her yet."

My sister grabs my hand, and this time I do break down. The tears burn in the cold.

The priest clears his throat; he's about to begin. In the distance the sounds of protestors grows louder, the rise and fall of their chants not unpleasant—though from this distance, thankfully, I cannot make out the words.

• • •

n-words

WHEN THE WORLD first learned of the Korean children, it sprang into action. Humanitarian groups swooped into the war-torn area, monies exchanged hands, and many of the children were adopted out to other countries—a new worldwide Diaspora. They were broad, thick-limbed children; usually slightly shorter than average, though there were startling exceptions to this.

They looked like members of the same family, and some of them, assuredly, were more closely related than that. There were more children, after all, than there were fossil specimens from which they'd derived. Duplicates were inevitable.

From what limited data remained of the Koreans' work, there had been more than sixty different DNA sources. Some even had names: the Old Man La Chappelle aux Saints, Shanidar IV and Vindija. There was the handsome and symmetrical La Ferrassie specimen. And even Amud I. *Huge* Amud I, who had stood 1.8 meters tall and had a cranial capacity of 1740ccs—the largest Neanderthal ever found.

The techniques perfected on dogs and mammoths had worked easily, too, within the genus Homo. Extraction, then PCR to amplify. After that came IVF with paid surrogates. The success rate was high, the only complication frequent cesarean births. And that was one of the things popular culture had to absorb, that Neanderthal heads were larger.

Tests were done. The children were studied and tracked and evaluated. All lacked normal dominant ex-

seeds of change

pression at the MC1R locus—all were pale-skinned, freckled, with red or blonde hair. All were blue-eyed. All were Rh negative.

I was six years old when I first saw a picture. It was the cover of *Time*—what is now a famous cover. I'd heard about these children but had never seen one—these children who were almost my age, from a place called Korea; these children that were sometimes called ghosts.

The magazine showed a pale, red-haired Neanderthal boy standing with his adoptive parents, staring thoughtfully up at an outdated anthropology display at a museum. The wax Neanderthal man in the display carried a club. He had a nose from the tropics, dark hair, olive-brown skin and dark brown eyes. Before Harding's child, the museum display designers had supposed they knew what primitive looked like, and they had supposed it was decidedly swarthy.

Never mind that Neanderthals had spent ten times longer in light-starved Europe than a typical Swede's ancestors.

The redheaded boy on the cover wore a confused expression.

When my father walked into the kitchen and saw the *Time* cover, he shook his head in disgust. "It's an abomination," he said.

I studied the boy's jutting face. I'd never seen anyone with face like that. "Who is he?"

"A dead-end. Those kids are going to be a drain for the rest of their lives. It's not fair to them, really."

N-words

That was the first of many pronouncements I'd hear about the children.

Years passed and the children grew like weeds—and as with all populations, the first generation exposed to a western diet grew several inches taller than their ancestors. While they excelled at sports, their adopted families were told they could be slow learners. They were primitive after all.

A prediction which turned out to be as accurate as the museum displays.

WHEN I LOOK up, the priest's hands are raised into the cold, white sky. "Blessed are you, O God our father; praised be your name forever." He breathes smoke, reading from the Book of Tobit.

It is a passage I've heard at both funerals and marriage ceremonies, and this, like the cold on this day, is fitting. "Let the heavens and all your creations praise you forever."

The mourners sway in the giant's breathing of the tent.

I was born Catholic, but found little use for organized religion in my adulthood. Little use for it, until now, when its use is so clearly revealed—and it is an unexpected comfort to be part of something larger than yourself; it is a comfort to have someone to bury your dead.

Religion provides a man in black to speak words over your loved one's grave. It does this first. If it does not do this, it is not religion.

seeds of change

"You made Adam and you gave him your wife Eve to be his love and support; and from these two, the human race descended."

They said together, *Amen, Amen.*

THE DAY I learned I was pregnant, David stood at our window, huge, pale arms draped over my shoulders. He touched my stomach as we watched a storm coming in across the lake.

"I hope the baby looks like you," he said in his strange, nasal voice.

"I don't."

"No, it would be easier if the baby looks like you. He'll have an easier life."

"He?"

"I think it's a boy."

"And is that what you'd wish for him, to have an easy life?"

"Isn't that what every parent wishes for?"

"No," I said. I touched my own stomach. I put my small hand over his large one. "I hope our son grows to be a good man."

I'D MET DAVID at Stanford when he walked into class five minutes late.

He had arms like legs. And legs like torsos. His torso was the trunk of an oak— seventy-five years old, grown in the sun. A full-sleeve tattoo swarmed up one bulging,

N-words

ghost-pale arm, disappearing under his shirt. He had an earring in one ear, and a shaved head. A thick red goatee balanced the enormous bulk of his convex nose and gave some dimension to his receding chin. The eyes beneath his thick brows were large and intense—as blue as a husky's.

It wasn't that he was handsome, because I couldn't decide if he was. It was that I couldn't take my eyes off him. I stared at him. All the girls stared at him.

It was harder for them to get into graduate programs back then. There were quotas—and like Asians, they had to score better to get accepted.

There was much debate over what name should go next to the race box on their entrance forms. The word "Neanderthal" had evolved into an epithet over the previous decade. It became just another N-word polite society didn't use.

I'd been to the clone rights rallies. I'd heard the speakers. "The French don't call themselves Cro-Magnons, do they?" the loudspeakers boomed.

And so the name by their box had changed every few years, as the college entrance questionnaires strove to map the shifting topography of political correctness. Every few years, a new name for the group would arise—and then a few years later sink again under the accumulated freight of prejudice heaped upon it.

They were called Neanderthals at first, then archaics, then clones—then, ridiculously, they were called simply Koreans, since that was the country in which all but one of

seeds of change

them had been born. Sometime after the word "Neanderthal" became an epithet, there was a movement by some militants within the group to reclaim the word, to use it within the group as a sign of strength.

But over time, the group gradually came to be known exclusively by a name that had been used occasionally from the very beginning, a name which captured the hidden heart of their truth. Among their own kind, and finally, among the rest of the world, they came to be known as the ghosts. All the other names fell away, and here, finally, was a name that stayed.

IN 2033, THE first ghost was drafted into the NFL. He spoke three languages. By 2035, the front line of every team in the league had one—*had* to have one, to be competitive. In the 2036 Olympics, ghosts took gold in wrestling, in power lifting, in almost every event in which they were entered. Some individuals took golds in multiple sports, in multiple areas.

There was an outcry from the other athletes who could not hope to compete. There were petitions to have ghosts banned from competition. It was suggested they should have their own Olympics, distinct from the original. Lawyers for the ghosts pointed out, carefully, tactfully, that out of the fastest 400 times recorded for the 100 yard dash, 386 had been achieved by persons of at least partial sub-Saharan African descent, and nobody was suggesting *they* get their own Olympics.

N-words

Of course, racist groups like the KKK and the neo-Nazis actually liked the idea, and proposed just that. Blacks, too, should compete against their own kind, get their own Olympics. After that, the whole matter degenerated into chaos.

WHEN I WAS growing up, I helped my grandfather prune his apple trees in Indiana. The trick, he told me, was telling which branches helped the fruit, and which branches didn't. Once you've studied a tree, you got a sense of what was important. Everything else you could cut away as useless baggage.

You can discard your ethnic identity through a similar process of careful ablation. You look at your child's face, and you don't wonder whose side you're on. You know.

I read in a sociology book that when someone in the privileged majority marries a minority, they take on the social status of that minority group. It occurred to me how the universe is a series of concentric circles, and you keep seeing the same shapes and processes wherever you look. Atoms are little solar systems; highways are a nation's arteries, streets its capillaries—and the social system of humans follows Mendelian genetics, with dominants and recessives. Minority ethnicity is the dominant gene when part of a heterozygous couple.

THERE ARE MANY Neanderthal bones in the Field Museum.

seeds of change

Their bones are different than ours. It is not just their big skulls, or their short, powerful limbs; virtually every bone in their body is thicker, stronger, heavier. Each vertebrae, each phalange, each small bone in the wrist, is thicker than ours. And I have wondered sometimes, when looking at those bones, why they need skeletons like that. All that metabolically expensive bone and muscle and brain. It had to be paid for. What kind of life makes you need bones like chunks of rebar? What kind of life makes you need a sternum half an inch thick?

During the Pleistocene, glaciers had carved their way south across Europe, isolating animal populations behind a curtain of ice. Those populations either adapted to the harsh conditions, or they died. Over time, the herd animals grew massive, becoming more thermally efficient; and so began the age of the Pleistocene mega-fauna. The predators too, had to adapt. The saber-tooth cat, the cave bear. They grew more powerful in order to bring down the larger prey. What was true for other animals was true for genus *Homo*, nature's experiment, the Neanderthal—the region's ultimate climax predator.

THREE DAYS AGO, the day David died, I woke to an empty bed. I found him naked at the window in our living room, looking out into the winter sky, his leonine face wrapped in shadow.

From behind, I could see the V of his back against the gray light. I knew better than to disturb him. He became a silhouette against the sky, and in that instant, he was something more and less than human—like some broad human creature adapted for life in extreme gravity. A person built to survive stresses that would crush a normal man.

He turned look at me. "There's a storm coming today," he said.

THE DAY DAVID died, I woke to an empty bed. I wonder about that.

I wonder if he suspected something. I wonder what got him out of bed early. I wonder at the storm he mentioned, the one he said was coming.

If he'd known the risk, we never would have gone to the rally—I'm sure of that, because he was a cautious man. But I wonder if some hidden, inner part of him didn't have its ear to the railroad tracks; I wonder if some part of him didn't feel the ground shaking, didn't hear the freight train barreling down on us all.

We ate breakfast that morning. We drove to the babysitter's and dropped off our son. David kissed him on the cheek and tousled his hair. There was no last look, no sense this would be the final time. David kissed the boy, tousled his hair, and then we were out the door, Mary waving goodbye.

We drove to the hall in silence. We parked our car in the crowded lot, ignoring the counter-rally already forming across the street.

We shook hands with other guests and found our way

seeds of change

to the assigned table. It was supposed to be a small luncheon, a civilized affair between moneyed men in expensive suits. David was the second speaker.

Up on the podium, David's expression changed. Before his speeches, there was this moment, this single second, where he glanced out over the crowd, and his eyes grew sad.

David closed his eyes, opened them, and spoke. He began slowly. He spoke of the flow of history and the symmetry of nature. He spoke of the arrogance of ignorance; and in whispered tones, he spoke of fear. "And out of fear," he said. "grows hatred." He let his eyes wander over the crowd. "They hate us because we're different," he said, voice rising for the first time. "Always it works this way, wherever you look in history. And always we must work against it. We must never give in to violence. But we are right to fear, my friends. We must be vigilant, or we'll lose everything we've gained for our children, and our children's children." He paused.

I'd heard this speech before, or parts of it. David rarely used notes, preferring to pull the speeches out of his head, assembling an oratorical structure both delicate and profound. He continued for another ten minutes before finally going into his close.

"They've talked about restricting us from athletic competition. They've eliminated us from receiving most scholarships. They've limited our attendance of law schools, and medical schools, and PhD programs. These are the soft shackles they've put upon us, and we cannot sit silently and let it happen."

The crowd erupted into applause. David lifted his hands to silence them and he walked back to his seat. Other speakers took the podium, but none with David's eloquence. None with his power.

When the last speaker sat, dinner was brought out and we ate. An hour later, when the plates were clean, more hands were shaken, and people started filing out to their cars. The evening was over.

David and I took our time, talking with old friends, but we eventually worked our way into the lobby. Ahead of us, out in the parking lot, there was a commotion. The counter-rally had grown. Somebody mentioned vandalized cars, and then Tom was leaning into David's ear, whispering as we passed through the front doors and out into the open air.

It started with thrown eggs. Thomas turned, egg-white drooling down his broad chest. The fury in his eyes was enough to frighten me. David rushed forward and grabbed his arm. There was a look of surprise on some of the faces in the crowd, because even they hadn't expected anybody to throw things—and I could see, too, the group of young men, clumped together near the side of the building, eggs in hand, mouths open—and it was like time stopped, because the moment was fat and waiting—and it could go any way, and an egg came down out of the sky that was not an egg, but a rock, and it struck Sarah Mitchell

seeds of change

in the face—and the blood was red and shocking on her ghost-white skin, and the moment was wide open, time snapping back the other way—everything moving too fast, all of it happening at the same time instead of taking turns the way events are supposed to. And suddenly David's grip on my arm was a vise, physically lifting me, pulling me back toward the building, and I tried to keep my feet while someone screamed.

"Everybody go back inside!" David shouted. And then another woman screamed, a different kind of noise, like a shout of warning—and then I heard it, a shout that was a roar like nothing I'd ever heard before—and then more screams, men's screams. And somebody lunged from the crowd and swung at David, and he moved so quickly I was flung away, the blow missing David's head by a foot.

"No!" David yelled at the man. "We don't want this."

Then the man swung again and this time David caught the fist in his huge hand. He jerked the man close. "We're not doing this," he hissed and flung him back into the crowd.

David grabbed Tom's arm again, trying to guide him back toward the building. "This is stupid, don't be pulled into it."

Thomas growled and let himself be pulled along, and someone spit in his face, and I saw it, the dead look in his eyes, to be spit on and do nothing. And still David pulled us toward the safety of the building, brushing aside the curses of men whose necks he could snap. And still he did

N-words

nothing. He did nothing all the way up to the end, when a thin, balding forty-year-old man stepped into his path, raised a gun, and fired point blank into his chest.

THE BLAST WAS deafening.

—and that old sadness gone. Replaced by white-hot rage and disbelief, blue eyes wide.

People tried to scatter, but the crush of bodies prevented it. David hung there, in the crush, looking down at his chest. The man fired three more times before David fell.

"ASHES TO ASHES, dust to dust. Accept our brother David into your warm embrace." The priest lowers his hands and closes the bible. The broad casket is lowered into the ground. It is done.

Dr. Michaels carries the boy as my sister helps me back to the limo.

THE NIGHT DAVID was killed, after the hospital and the police questions, I drove to the sitter's to pick up my son. Mary hugged me and we stood crying in the foyer for a long time.

"What do I tell my two-year old?" I said. "How do I explain this?"

We walked to the front room, and I stood in the doorway. I watched my son like I was seeing him for the first time. He was blocky, like his father, but his bones were longer. He was a gifted child who knew his letters and could already sound out certain words.

And that was our secret, that he was not yet three and already learning to read. And there were thousands more like him—a new generation, the best of two tribes.

Perhaps David's mistake was that he hadn't realized there was a war. In any war, there are only certain people who fight it—and a smaller number who understand, truly, *why* it's being fought. This was no different.

Sixty thousand years ago, there were two walks of men in the world. There were the people of the ice, and there were the people of the sun.

When the climate warmed, the ice sheets retreated. The broad African desert was beaten back by the rains, and the people of the sun expanded north.

The world was changing then. The European megafauna were disappearing. The delicate predator/prey equilibrium slipped out of balance and the world's most deadly climax predator found his livelihood evaporating in warming air. Without the big herds, there was less food. The big predators gave way to sleeker models that needed fewer calories to survive.

The people of the sun weren't stronger, or smarter, or better than the people of the ice; Cain didn't kill his brother, Abel. The snow people didn't die out because they weren't good enough. All that bone and muscle and brain. They died because they were too expensive.

But now the problems are different. Now the world

has changed again. Again there are two kinds of men in the world. But in this new age, it will not be the economy version of man who wins.

THE LIMO DOOR slams shut. The vehicle pulls away from the grave. As we near the cemetery gates, the shouting grows louder. The protestors see us coming.

The police said that David's murder was a crime of passion. Others said he was a target of opportunity. I don't know which is true. The truth died with the shooter, when Tom crushed his skull with a single right-hand blow.

The shouting spikes louder as we pass the cemetery gates. A snowball smashes into the window.

"Stop the car!" I shout.

I fling open the door. I climb out and walk up to the surprised man. He's standing there, another snowball already packed in his hands. I'm not sure what I'm going to do as I approach him. I've gotten used to the remarks, the small attacks. I've gotten used to ignoring them. I've gotten used to saying nothing.

I slap him in the face as hard as I can.

He's too shocked to react at first. I slap him again.

This time he flinches away from me, wanting no part of this. I walk back to my car as people start screaming at me. I climb in and the limo driver pulls away.

My son looks at me, and it's not fear in his eyes like I expect; it's anger. Anger at the crowd. My huge, brilliant son—these people have no idea what they're doing. They have no idea the storm they're calling down.

I see a sign held high as we pass the last of the protestors. They are shouting again, having found the full flower of their outrage. The sign says only one word: *Die.*

Not this time, I think to myself. *Your turn.*

the future by degrees
> > >

Jay Lake is the author of three novels, with several more in the pipeline. He is also the author of more than 200 short stories, which have appeared in magazines such as Realms of Fantasy, Asimov's, *and* Interzone. *He is a winner of the John W. Campbell Award for Best New Writer, and was a first place winner in the L. Ron Hubbard Writers of the Future contest. He's also been a finalist for both the Hugo and World Fantasy Awards.*

Lake said "The Future by Degrees" was inspired by his fascination with thermal superconductivity. "Seeds of Change looked like the perfect market to tackle the topic directly, given that such a concept would be just about the most profound revolution ever seen in technology," Lake said. "Think about how much of the design of any electronic device is concerned with waste heat management. Likewise internal combustion engines. Or the heat transfer issues in climate control within residences and commercial buildings. The list is endless."

the future
by degrees
Jay Lake

"It's a simple concept, really."

Grover hated public speaking. Which was ironic, given his job in sales development for Quantum Thermal Systems. A half-empty church basement full of metal folding chairs was a special nightmare. He could hear his voice echoing off the metal half-moons topping each vacant seat, so that there was a metallic ring just a fraction of a beat behind his words. Debris punctuated the scuffed linoleum floor:

the future by degrees

candy wrappers, folded over flyers, and—improbably enough in the function room of the Second Methodist Church—a torn condom wrapper.

The chairs were mostly empty, the rest populated by a bored collection of farmers, ranchers and small town businessmen. Most were already nodding off, the rest sat in exaggerated poses of doubt, like a particularly truculent line of Hummel figurines. Salt of the earth, his mother would have called these men. Salty old bastards, more like it.

There were no women present this evening.

Grover held up his model. It was built from styrene sheets bought on sale at Hobbytown, glued to a styrofoam core with a few strategic wires dangling out of one end, simply because nobody ever believed in a prototype without exposed copper. The whole thing was spray painted matte black, with a bit of silvery duct tape for added effect. Any engineer knew what a casing was — skin for the reality within, bearing no more relationship to performance than the line of an automobile's fender did to the drive train.

People, though, regular people who went to work every day and drove pickup trucks and had trouble balancing their checkbooks . . . they needed to see the semblance of a thing before they could understand the reality beneath the skin. Farmers knew their nitrogen from their phosphates, but physical chemistry was as foreign to these people as Russian literature or Indonesian *rijsttafel*.

seeds of change

Damn it, he thought. His mind was wandering again.

"This little device," he said, then stopped to clear his throat. *Try again.* Pale, pasty and too fat to look authoritative, Grover had to rely on the words. He didn't have the convincing manner of a born salesman like Brody in the San Mateo office, and he'd never mastered the art of dressing his inconveniently round belly to look anything but sloppy-pudgy.

"This little device will save you more trouble and money than you could ever have thought possible."

He spun the prototype in his hands.

"The production model will weight about twenty pounds. It will cost you about a hundred dollars. It will store about 18,000,000 joules of heat."

Grover paused, took a deep breath.

"That's one day of peak thermal output of a cubic yard of fresh horse manure as it begins to compost. The equivalent of almost 800 kilowatt hours of electricity, the energy an average American household uses in a month. All of it with a loss of less than one percent efficiency per month."

The collective yawn was palpable. Chair legs scraped as some of the men gathered their weight to walk away. But he could see two or three chins tilted, two or three thoughtful looks.

Two or three people who understood what this thing would mean!

"It's called thermal superconductivity," Grover told them. The real details were a closely guarded secret, but

the future by degrees

the idea . . . the idea was priceless. "The future is here in our hands, if you can just imagine what this will do. The world has never seen anything like it. Not since the discovery of fire."

"THIS MATERIAL HAS two states," said Minnie. "Balanced and gradiated."

Grover shifted in his chair. The PowerPoints were either overly detailed or mysteriously vague. Or maybe it was just Minnie. He could imagine her hair undone from its bun, floating in wiry curls around that sensuous face.

Who knew Puerto Rican girls were so hot? Especially physical chemists.

"We've got the gradiated state working now," she went on. "It's in the form of a textile, for ease of manufacture and use. In the near future we'll have rigid forms with high ductility for applications requiring shaping or specific topologies. Transfer rates aren't optimal, but even now we can keep up with domestic uses. We're not far from internal combustion engine temperature ranges.

"As for the balanced state, I can't tell you much more than to say we expect it to be stable and replicable before the end of the next fiscal quarter."

As an engineer, he was lost among the sworn-to-NDA money men in the room. Grover's job was sales development for the product. Minnie's job was product development itself, and the high level sell of the concept.

And, well, to finish inventing it.

seeds of change

"The gradiated state moves heat. It's that simple. Flow direction, intensity and maxima are governed by extremely low voltage electrical inputs which realign the channeled carbon nanostructures."

The room was quiet, with the intensity of a dozen pairs of ears straining toward the biggest payoff in the history of venture capital.

"She means we can turn it off and on," Grover offered in a quiet voice. He'd taken a few yards of the lab castoffs home to play with, on the Q.T. Sales development, after all. Plus maybe a meaningful prototype, if he could get clearance for that. And it *was* cool as hell, even if the thermal gradiation was uncontrollably locked into place on the stuff he had. "Like a faucet. Hot, cold, trickle, flood."

"Right." Minnie made a face at him, somewhere between sweet and prissy. "That's very, very useful, but it's only a form of transference."

"So . . . " said one of the money men in a thoughtful voice. "We could remove the car's radiator, but the block heat still has to go somewhere."

"Right." She smiled, warming Grover's heart. "That's where the balanced state comes into play. Think of it as a really big sponge, storing that block heat until we want to let it out again."

That elided a lot of detail, but the real nut and bolts of this process were still burn-before-reading secret.

"What do we do with the heat later?" asked the money man.

the future by degrees

"Anything you want," Grover said. "Heat is power. Power is everything. The entire energy production and consumption system begins to feed itself, increasing our efficiencies dramatically across the society. Hell, this thing could have a net effect on global warming. It'd be nice to have Key West back, huh?"

There was a scatter of nervous laughter. Someone behind him stage whispered, "The Caymans, too. I had money there."

"Gentlemen," said Minnie in a tone of voice that made it clear that Grover's role as a shill was done. "What Quantum Thermal Systems does is all about the money. Saving the world is just a bonus."

GROVER'S IPHONE PRO rang. It took him a minute to disentangle from dreams of fire alarms and swimming pools filled with warm Kool-Aid, but he managed to slap the phone off the table onto his mattress and mash it to his ear.

"Grove, it's Brody." The sales manager sounded panicked. "Is that you?"

"Me?" Grover wasn't sure who else it would be. He was supposed to have been in Cleveland, but Wei Ming had taken that trip because Grover's allergies were acting up. Still, he never had a house sitter.

Brody's voice caught. "Take your prototypes and get out. Drive. Away. Borrow someone else's car."

"Wha . . . ?"

"The office just got whacked. Dorsey says it was a

seeds of change

Blackwater contract job. Whole building's in flames. Somebody ran Minnie off the road, snatched her, and took everything she had in her vehicle. Wei Ming's hotel room got tossed in Cleveland, he's in the ER there beat all to shit. There were two guys trying to break into my place just now, but I got out."

Shit. Allergy meds or not, Grover was suddenly very, very awake. They'd joked about this around the office, called it the Silkwood Scenario, after that poor woman killed by the nuclear power industry back in the 1970s for blowing the whistle. *What if Exxon came gunning for us? What if Con Ed sent out the utility ninjas?*

It wasn't a joke any more.

He scrambled out of bed, dragged himself into sweats, and stumbled down the short hall to his office.

Someone was standing in there, silhouetted in the streetlight glare through the window overlooking Circular Avenue. The figure's hand came up.

Grover's next thought arrived with utter clarity. *I'm going to die now.*

"Get in here," Minnie hissed.

A hard, nauseating ripple of shock twisted through Grover. "What?"

"I thought you were *dead* in Cleveland. Then I heard your damned phone ring."

"Dead? Me?" He tried to grapple with the obvious question. "What the hell are you doing in my house? Brody says—"

the future by degrees

"Brody's working for *them*." Her breath heaved, ragged and rough on the edge of collapsing from stress.

"Con Ed?"

She blinked. "What?"

"Sorry, sorry." He sneezed. "Allergy meds."

"Shut up." She picked up a satchel which had been on the floor by his desk. "Let's go."

Grover grabbed her arm. "What are you doing *here?*"

"Looking for that prototype battery you like to haul around. That, and your laptop."

Something wasn't adding up yet. Actually, everything wasn't adding up yet. "Did you find them?"

"Yes. Now let's *go*."

In the other room, his phone began ringing again.

"Minnie, if you believed I was dead in Cleveland, why did you think my laptop would be here?"

The phone rolled to voicemail, then started ringing again a few seconds later.

"Desperate times, Grove." She slugged him hard, then kicked him in the nuts as he collapsed. "Good luck with your house fire."

HE FOUND HIMSELF on his hands and knees. The damned iPhone was still ringing in the other room, with that digitized jangly 1960s payphone bell he used to think was so funny. Grover smelled smoke.

The alarms weren't chirping, though.

Painfully, he looked up. His vision was swimming in

doubled circles, but that was enough to see that the smoke alarm in his office had been yanked out of the ceiling.

Where's the fire?

Minnie had left him for dead. He wasn't walking out of here, that was for sure. Weren't you supposed to crawl in a fire, anyway?

Grover slid over to the office door and peeked underneath. There was flickering orange light in the hallway. His office window opened onto view of rose bushes and a spike-topped iron fence at the back of the condo complex. Better than being burnt to death, maybe, but not much.

I am going to die now.

He was tired of that thought already. He keeled over onto his side, tried to keep from crying, then wondered why he cared if he cried. His eyes were running freely with the burn from the smoke.

Instead Grover thought about Minnie. What the hell was she doing? Brody had thought she was dead. QTS was gone in a night of murder and flames.

She'd said it was all about the money. Someone must have offered her a ridiculous amount to take the product and disappear.

An amount so ridiculous she'd kill for it?

The phone finally stopped ringing. Smoke was creeping under the door, sending gray fingers up to the ceiling. Grover's midsection no longer felt like it had gone nova, but he was stuck here. His only hope was that the fire department arrived before the fire did.

the future by degrees

No sirens yet.

A thought made him sit upright, which in turn brought an unpleasant rush to his head. She'd been here looking for his dummy prototype. *She hadn't known he'd taken the defective samples home.*

"I'm going to live," Grover told the fire.

He dropped to all fours again and crawled to the closet. It was full of supplies, winter clothes, the sort of crap that a bedroom-turned-office accumulated. He'd tossed his sweaters back in there after dropping out of the Cleveland trip. Underneath them was four yards of strangely slick black cloth, so dark it looked like a hole in the shadows of the closet. Eighteen inches wide, twelve feet long. Enough to wrap himself like a mummy and walk out through the fire.

So long as he got the gradiation right. It would do him no good for the nanostructures to pipe all the heat of the fire *inward* to his skin.

Power still seemed to be working, even with the fire. Grover tugged his lamp off the desk, switched on the bulb, and set the cloth against it to see which side got hot and which side stayed cool.

"YOU CAN'T HOLD me," Grover said. "And I'm going public as soon as I find a reporter." *Or a phone, at least,* he amended.

Special Agent Angela Looks Twice stared him down. "I'm not going to let you walk out that door." The compact woman from the FBI was currently in the grip of fury. Grover was perfectly willing to believe she could take him apart, joint by joint if required.

They were crowded together in the manager's office of the Denny's two blocks away from his condo complex. The complex had gone four alarms last he heard. He and the agent were crammed into a tiny room arranged for the convenience of one person. The manager clearly spent a lot of time trying to motivate low-wage workers through old fashioned intimidation, at least judging by the posters on the wall warning of all the different ways a job could be lost.

"Everyone connected with Quantum Thermal Systems is missing or dead." She stabbed a finger at him. "Your colleague in Cleveland. Brody. At least four innocent bystanders that we know of. Everyone. Except you."

"Right." Grover felt a laugh welling up inside him. He swallowed it hard. "You're never going to suck this thing down the memory hole now. Hell, I must have spoken to four or five dozen groups in past six months. A lot of investors heard the pitch. Now you're going to have victim's families asking questions."

"You'd be amazed what gets sucked down the memory hole." Looks Twice had a grim smile on her face. "You walked out of a 1100 degree fire with normal skin and core temps. The defense applications of this thing alone are worth a total blackout."

"Not to mention the firefighting applications," Grover said sarcastically. "I don't care what the hell you do with it.

the future by degrees

It just can't stay secret. That's what all the killing, all the fires are about. Covering it up. Making it go away. Just another failed startup. Except most startups don't end in a series of murders and kidnappings."

Looks Twice rubbed her temples, then gave him a long, slow look. "Ever hear of Heaven's Gate? Cults make great cover for this kind of operation. Everybody spends a minute feeling sorry for the dead whack jobs, then moves on."

"Got a lot better at it since Karen Silkwood, huh?" Grover stood up. "Arrest me, or let me go."

Her fists clenched. "I can hold you as a material witness."

Grover grabbed the doorknob. When had he ever fought back like this? *Maybe since people died tonight.* "Or you can help me ... "

"Don't open the door, Mr. Ruggles. There are a number of pissed off cops out there who will stop you. They might even check with me, after you're finished resisting arrest."

"So, arrest me now or let me go."

"And you'll walk out and find a reporter? I can promise you, anyone with the resources to coordinate this many assaults and arsons in one evening will have no trouble finishing the job with respect to you. Any interview you go to will be the last thing you ever do."

"Then help me stay alive long enough to go public," Grover said with a growl. He wondered where all this courage was coming from, and how soon it would evapo-

seeds of change

rate. "Go so public it won't matter. Fuck the NDAs. There's no one left to sue me for violating them."

He leaned over her desk, being as persuasive as he knew how. *Do it for Brody*, he thought. *For Wei Ming. For all of them.*

"I didn't invent this stuff, but I can explain it well enough that people with the right training will know what to do to recreate it. If thirty or forty universities and corporate labs nationwide are working on it, there's not much point in killing to keep the secret. I'll make the memory hole so damned big that even Karl Rove couldn't disappear this thing. Hell, once the Chinese or the Russians start working on the knock-offs, the QTS tech will be worldwide. And it will change the world."

Looks Twice snorted with a rueful amusement. "You don't think small, do you?"

"Almost all the time," he admitted. "I'm a small kind of guy. Just not this time. I walked through fire, remember? Think about what else that stuff will do."

The last remnants of anger seemed to leave Special Agent Looks Twice in a heaving rush. She pulled a business card from her jacket pocket. "You're free to go, Mr. Ruggles. Call me if you think of anything. I suggest you don't leave town without talking to the District Attorney."

Grover was surprised. He'd always figured FBI agents for world class hard asses when it came to law and order. That was pretty much the job description, after all. He gathered up the oversized plastic bag into which someone

the future by degrees

had stuffed the strips of thermal superconductor. The plastic was bubbled and stretched from residual heat.

"Mr. Ruggles," Looks Twice said tentatively as he pulled open the door.

Grover turned around, a state wage-and-hour poster looming large in his peripheral vision. "Yes, ma'am?"

"My mother and my baby brother died when our trailer burned. A lot of years ago. I find a ... special pleasure in investigating arsons." She took another deep, ragged breath. "If they'd been able to walk through fire ... "

"Sometimes it *is* all about saving the world," he said.

GROVER WAS ON local television the next morning. The reporter loaned him her cell phone as he left the studio, and promised to give out the number to everyone she could think of who might be interested.

Within an hour, driving a rented Focus hybrid along a random set of roads through the Willamette Valley, he took calls from reporters from the *San Jose Mercury News*, the *New York Times* and *Agence France-Presse*. He couldn't do anything about the cell phone being traced except to keep moving.

Around noon he stopped at the public library in Silverton, then went by the local post office to mail samples of the thermal superconducting cloth to every major university he could think of. First class, no tracking, paid for in cash. That was as anonymous as he could think to make the process of getting the stuff out into the world.

seeds of change

After mailing off the samples, he drove east into the Cascades. One of the *Mercury News* reporters called back with home number of a science fiction author who was also an "A" list blogger and a feature writer for *Wired*. Grover called and told his story. The writer immediately grasped the implications of the idea, in both states — gradiated and balanced. "Waste heat alone," he said. "You're on the way to providing a manageable approach to global warming, and closing a huge portion of the loop on power generation. Those are two of the biggest stumbling blocks on the Kardashev scale."

"It's still lossy," Grover said, guessing at what the other man was talking about. "We can't escape the Laws of Thermodynamics."

"Right, but you're going from maybe thirty percent thermal efficiency on internal combustion to, what, ninety-five percent? Or more. You just keep reusing it." The writer sounded thrilled. "It's the future by degrees. This has applications everywhere. Did you know that they put air conditioners in equipment shacks in North Slope Alaska? Forty below outside, and a compressor running inside the insulation to manage the heat rise. This stuff . . . "

The conversation spun off into space exploration, medicine, environmental remediation, the potential for home-based power generation from waste heat, before the mountains ate the cell phone signal. Grover laughed at the waste heat idea, thinking back on his manure pile analogy.

• • •

the future by degrees

THE SILKWOOD SQUAD caught up with him just on the eastern side of Santiam Pass. Grover was surprised to have gotten even that far.

A helicopter with no markings, not even a tail number, was parked on the highway. He could see a large yellow dump truck at a curve half a mile downhill. They were roadblocking any potential witnesses.

Minnie stood in front of the helicopter, wrapped in an oversized windbreaker. Somehow she didn't seem so beautiful to him any more. There were three men with her. They were bulky, in gray suits and dark glasses. It was a scene straight out of Central Casting. Grover found the sheer lack of imagination offensive.

He pulled the car over and got out. "It's a rental," he shouted, feeling light-headed. Minnie's fire had finally caught up to him. "Probably don't need to blow it up."

Minnie nodded. "We tracked you by the car company's GPS."

"The secret is blown." Grover took a couple of steps toward Minnie. "It's all over the world now. Not the sales hokum we've been passing this whole time. The real thing, as much as I had of it. Including samples." His knees quivered. "You can shoot me now, like you did Brody and Wei Ming, but it doesn't matter any more."

"Hmm." She flicked her hand and the big men came for Grover.

"I saved the world," he shouted just before the first blow landed hard enough to crack his jaw.

seeds of change

Minnie's voice was distinct over the grinding thump of brass knuckles and tape-wrapped pipes. "And you pissed away a hell of a lot of money doing it."

THE BIGGEST SURPRISE was that they let him live. A long haul trucker had found Grover by the side of the road, and called in the EMTs, who'd evacuated him by helicopter. Now he sat in a Salem hospital, aching at every joint. His right eye had a detached retina and his left was full of blood.

Something moved in the doorway. Grover squinted, mumbling, "Who's there?"

"Special Agent Looks Twice," said the blur.

"Oh, hey." At least, that's what Grover tried to say.

"Don't talk. I just thought I'd tell you there's no air traffic control record on a helicopter near the Santiam Pass. No one saw anything coming and going. So far as the Jefferson County sheriff's department is concerned, you drove up there alone and tried to commit suicide."

"Beat myself to death?"

"I believe the press was told you'd thrown yourself off the top of a road cut and sustained injuries striking the cliff on the way down." She stood close enough to the bed that he could see her.

Grover fought to make the next words clear. "And the thermal cloth?"

"Front page news, pretty much everywhere." He thought she might have smiled. "You won."

the future by degrees

"Heat is the engine of the world." He knew that wouldn't make sense to her, not through his shattered mouth.

"Right. I've got to go." Looks Twice stroked his arm briefly. "Hey, firewalker. They ever let you out of here, give me a call sometime."

Grover lay back, imagining what the future might be like.

drinking problem

> > >

K.D. Wentworth is a three-time finalist for the Nebula Award, and is the author of seven novels. Her most recent is The Course of Empire *and she is currently working on a sequel. She is also the author of more than seventy short stories, which have appeared in magazines such as* The Magazine of Fantasy & Science Fiction, Realms of Fantasy, Weird Tales, *and elsewhere.*

Wentworth said that "Drinking Problem" concerns a man who runs afoul of a new technology intended to cut down on the need to recycle. But, as with many innovations, the technology has unintended consequences.

drinking problem

k.d. wentworth

oe settled into his accustomed seat before the Brass Tack's polished black granite bar. It had been a tough day, full of stupid meetings. But, hey, lots of days were tough. Nothing new there. The jukebox was grinding out something unmelodic and off to one side, a frizzy-headed woman regarded the beer bottle in the middle of her table with dread

drinking problem

as though it was about to explode. Outside, the July sun was blazing, even at 5:30 a force with which to be reckoned.

"Cold one?" Tom Whitebear, the barkeep asked. He was tall, black-haired, and laconic with the presence of a deep dark well, absorbing his patrons' words and giving back blessed silence.

Joe nodded, liking that he didn't even have to ask. His tongue was already full of holes from biting it all day long. If Salinger emailed him one more time demanding reports that weren't even due yet, by God, he would take a stapler to the idiot's balding head.

Tom slid a bottle with a strange blue and gold label in front of him and stared at it morosely.

"I drink *Miller*," Joe said, too weary to raise his voice.

"This *is* Miller," Tom said, sliding a slip of paper across the gleaming blackness. "The packaging's just different. They call it a 'Smart Bottle.' Even comes with its own instructions."

"Instructions for a freaking bottle of beer?" Joe blinked.

Tom seized a cloth and buffed the bar as though it was smeared—which it wasn't. "You been in Tibet or something? Press has been screaming about this for weeks. It's the law, went into effect today. Brew's only available in these fancy 'Smart' bottles now. Supposed to save the environment. Big Brother watching out for us and all that."

"I don't get it." Joe flicked the back of his finger against the cold glass, making it ring. The label featured a man holding up a bottle and smiling broadly.

seeds of change

"Whole damn country, no, make that the whole damned world, is going to hell." Tom peeled off a tab below the label that ran all around the bottle and pushed it gingerly toward him with his fingertips. "Joe Browder, meet your Smart Bottle," he said in an oddly formal way, as though he were introducing Joe to a potential partner at a stupid speed-dating party.

Joe noticed belatedly that the barkeep was pulling off latex gloves. "What the hell?"

"Hope the two of you will be very happy," Tom muttered and slouched off to wait on a man at the far end of the bar.

Joe picked the bottle up, finding the label's texture oddly rough. His hand tingled and he set the bottle aside to examine his palm. The skin was slightly reddened as though he'd scraped it against something.

"Greetings!" a hollow little voice said. "I am your Symesco A2300 Smart Bottle equipped with DNA recognition software and a high environmental consciousness quotient. I will be handling all your future beer consumption needs."

Joe pushed back off the stool, his heart thumping. "Did that thing just talk?"

"Drink me, Joe," the bottle said, "while I'm nice and frosty. Delay will not improve the esthetics of the experience."

Hairs crawled on the back of his neck. "Like hell I will!"

drinking problem

"Might as well," Tom said as he came back. "Once you touch the sensor, infernal thing is imprinted on you. It's yours—permanently."

Fuming, Joe threw a five on the bar and stood.

"Actually, it costs twenty-five bucks." Tom pushed it toward him. "One-time deposit. And you take it with you so I can refill it the next time you come in."

Joe pulled a twenty out of his billfold and added it to the five, glaring at the offending bottle with its ridiculous blue and gold label. "Not in this lifetime, buddy!" He turned to go.

"I wouldn't do that if I were you," Tom said to his back. "Damn thing has a proximity sensor."

Joe was halfway to the door when the racket began, sort of like a tornado siren augmented by the agonies of a dying cat. The closer he got to the door, the louder it became. The other patrons were holding their hands over their ears and appeared to be shouting at him, but he couldn't hear them. Tom seized the bottle and followed him to the door. "You got to take it with you," he said, "or it won't let up!"

Joe snatched the bottle and the moment he touched it, the clamor cut off. At a side table, a man and woman, both in their twenties, shook their heads. "Dumb-ass," the man, who looked like one of those fresh-faced business school grads, said. "Didn't read the instructions, did you?"

Joe had a half a mind to break the bottle over the sod's head. Tom retrieved the abandoned operating sheet and

seeds of change

pushed it into Joe's other hand. "You need to familiarize yourself with the bad news," he said in a low voice. "I'm afraid things are going to be very different around here."

Joe stuffed the paper into his pocket and stalked out.

JOE POURED OUT the bottle on the sidewalk and drove his Mazda home to his apartment. Terri was waiting with lasagna in the oven. She worked as a third grade teacher so she arrived home first. Unfortunately, she always wanted to natter at him about how exhausting *her* day had been the second he got home, so that he never had a quiet moment to put his thoughts in order.

"What's that?" she said as he closed the door.

"Something called a 'Smart Bottle,' " he said, setting it down with a thump on the breakfast bar. He dropped his briefcase onto the coffee table and wrenched at his tie. "The bartender tricked me into buying it at the Brass Tack."

"My class read about these," she said, picking it up and turning it under the light to examine the label. "They're supposed to cut down on the need to recycle."

"Actually, Symesco Smart Bottles cannot be recycled," the hollow little voice said. "We are engineered with DNA recognition software to provide years of imbibing pleasure."

Joe sank onto the couch. "I can't get the stupid thing to shut up."

"Why do you have DNA recognition capabilities?" Terri said.

drinking problem

"I am Joe's bottle," it said. "If I could not recognize him, I might be employed by any number of unauthorized users. That would be unhygienic."

"Correction," Joe said, taking the bottle out of Terri's hand. "You *were* my bottle. Now you're just so much scrap glass." He opened the pantry and tossed the bottle with a clank into the recycling bin.

The racket began again, this time much worse in the confined space of the apartment. Cursing, he pulled the bottle out. "Stop that!" The wail cut off.

Terri glared. "Did you pay good money for that thing?"

"Washington evidently passed some sort of stupid law when no one was paying attention," he muttered, then dug in his pocket for the wadded instructions. "But there must be a way to turn it off, otherwise, you'd have to take it to work with you and even in the shower."

"Congratulations on your purchase of a Symesco A2300 Smart Bottle," the instructions read, "The first monumental step toward maintaining a waste-free environment!"

He skimmed down through more bombastic, self-aggrandizing rhetoric, which included the instructions for removing the tab over the sensor and introducing the "client" to the bottle, until he reached "Temporary Deactivation."

"You can command your bottle to 'sleep' when not in use for twenty-four hours at a time," the instructions read.

seeds of change

"with one two-week deactivation permitted every four months when the client wishes to vacation without his Smart Bottle, though this is not recommended. It can be reactivated at any time by simply touching the DNA-sensitive label. Deactivation for longer or more frequent periods will require a waiver from Symesco. Those wishing to apply for the necessary code phrases should call the Symesco Help Line at 1-800-SMT-BOTL or consult our convenient website: www.symesco.com."

Joe held the brown bottle up. "Sleep, dammit!"

It didn't seem any different, but this time, when he tossed it into the recycling bin, it didn't protest.

Terri took the instructions and sat reading them until dinner was ready. They both ate in blessed silence.

WHEN HE SHOWED up at the Brass Tack the next day after work, Tom gave him a leery look. "Dude, where's your bottle?"

"In the recycling bin, where the damn thing belongs." Joe slid onto a stool and turned his palms down on the blessedly cool surface. "Bring me a cold one."

Tom folded his white bar cloth. "Can't."

"Are you trying to be funny?" Joe asked. "Because it's been a long frustrating day and I am in no way in the mood."

"It's against the law to serve registered Symesco users without their bottles," the barkeep said morosely. "You're at least the twentieth person I've had to tell that to since

drinking problem

noon. Can't nobody read instructions, I guess." He polished a bit of imaginary grime.

"And you registered me yesterday," Joe said. "Gee, thanks."

"It's the—"

"—law," Joe finished for him. "Okay, then sell me another stupid Smart Bottle." Though the thought of being responsible for two of the infernal devices was sobering, not the sensation he was seeking at the moment.

Tom shook his head. "One to a customer. It's the—"

Joe shoved away from the bar, knocking the stool over. "Guess I'll just take my business elsewhere!"

"Won't do no good," Tom said, studying his cleaning cloth. "No bar will serve you without checking identification, and you're in the system now as a Symesco user." He raised his head and met Joe's eyes. "Just go home and get your bottle and I'll refill the blasted thing until your eyes float."

But he didn't have time for that. Terri would have dinner on the table in thirty minutes and she would complain all night if he was late. "Forget it!" he said and plunged back outside into the glaring afternoon sun.

He stopped by the Pay-N-Git convenience store on the way home to pick up a six pack. The cooler was almost empty and he had to settle for an off-brand he'd never heard of, Bjorn's Mountain Gold. Probably tasted like yeast water.

The bored clerk, a narrow-eyed girl chomping on a wad of gum, gave him a stern look from behind the high counter. "ID?"

seeds of change

At thirty-seven, he hadn't been IDed for at least ten years, maybe more. He blinked. "You've got to be kidding."

"No, sir." She popped her gum and then jerked her chin to indicate the line of impatient customers behind him. "We never kid. It's like totally against company policy."

Sighing, he dug in his wallet and produced his driver's license. She punched in his number on a keypad, shook her head, and shoved the plastic rectangle back at him. "Sorry, pops, you're a registered Symesco user. I can't sell alternate containers to you." She gave him a hard-eyed look. "Even old geezers have to follow the rules, you know. If you have your bottle, we can refill it, but that's all."

Fuming, he relinquished the six pack and left.

HE HEARD THE wail before he got in the front door, the same high-pitched, ear-wrenching caterwaul. Jeeze, it hadn't been twenty-four hours yet, had it? He shoved his key in the lock and burst into their apartment.

Terri looked up from where she was pacing in a tight circle around the living room. She'd smothered the bottle in a blanket and shoved it under a sofa cushion, but that did little to muffle the monumental racket.

Her eyes were red and she wore the noise-canceling headphones she'd given him for Christmas. She'd crossed her arms protectively over her body as though warding off a blow. "Pick up the blasted thing before I lose my mind!"

drinking problem

she shouted. "The Super's already been up here complaining three times!"

He dug the blanket-swathed shape out from under the cushions and tore it free. As soon as his fingers touched the naked glass, the noise cut off.

"Hello, Joe," the bottle said companionably. "It's been over twenty-four hours since I was last filled. Shall we go out for a beer?"

Jeeze, the damn thing was going to turn him into an alcoholic! Heart racing, Joe hurled it against the wall. The plaster cracked but the bottle appeared unharmed.

"Fortunately, I am shatterproof," the bottle said from the corner where it had rolled. "Did you have a difficult day? I am programmed with sixteen modes of communication, including marital counseling and anger management. Let's talk it over."

Terri tore the headphones off her head with unsteady fingers. "I—I—want that thing out of here!"

Joe picked up the bottle and glared at it. "The instructions say you can 'sleep' for two weeks, right?" he said, feeling stupid talking to a freaking brown bottle.

"That is correct, but—"

"Then goddamn sleep for two weeks!"

Terri and Joe both studied the bottle, waiting for some indication that the command had worked, or hadn't. Finally he set it down on the coffee table and backed away. "I think that did it," he said softly as though it were a sleeping baby.

seeds of change

"For two weeks," she said. Her staring white-rimmed eyes hinted at future therapist bills. "Then it will be back in spades. My job is stressful enough. I can't take this!"

"Well," he said, slipping an arm around her shaking shoulders, "I wouldn't worry. In two long weeks, an awful lot can happen to a poor little bottle."

THE NEXT DAY was Saturday, so he rose early to take Terri and the bottle for a long ride in the countryside. He stopped finally at Roaring River State Park, where an underground river surfaced out of a split in the cliff, and deposited the bottle in one of the enormous bear-proof trash cans at a camping area. It was midmorning at that point, already getting hot, but they stood together before the can, hands entwined, savoring the moment. "We're free," Terri said fervently and he kissed her neck.

Then they returned home for a leisurely BBQ dinner at their favorite cafe. Things ran along quietly after that, the only problem being that he could no longer have a beer after work. He figured at some point, under-the-counter beer would be available from local drug dealers, but Smart Bottles were just catching on. It would take some time for illicit demand to develop.

He could have switched to whiskey or scotch, but he'd never been fond of the hard stuff. He just wanted fifteen minutes after work to sit in blessed silence and relax with a cold beer to take off the day's edge. Was that too much to ask?

drinking problem

Two weeks after he'd rid himself of the Smart Bottle—or Smart-ass Bottle, as he was coming to think of it—Joe stopped at the Brass Tack and ordered a Coke. "Want a shot of rum in that?" Tom Whitebear asked as he passed Joe the glass.

It had been a trying day. "Yeah, why not?" He shoved it back. "How's business since Smart Bottles became the law?"

"On that note, think I'll join you," Tom said, pouring himself a straight double shot of scotch.

"That's not good for you," a bottle chirped from back behind the bar. "You should—"

"Shut up or I'll stick you back in the freezer!" Tom said over his shoulder, then turned back to Joe. "My own Smart Bottle." He jerked his chin toward it. "I'm thinking of taking a hammer to the blasted thing."

"Won't do any good," Joe said, wrinkling his nose at the bite of the rum. "They're shatterproof."

"Heard one fellow threw his over Niagara Falls." Tom downed his scotch in a single swallow. His cheeks flushed.

"Did it work?" Joe asked with a prickle of hope.

"Nope." Tom regarded his empty glass as though it had answers. "Damned things float."

Joe thought of his own bottle, tucked away at this very moment in some faraway State landfill. Down under the ground, buried under layers of plastic garbage sacks and decomposing fries, it could holler all it wanted. He didn't care if he ever had another beer again if it meant he had to be a slave to a freaking computer chip.

seeds of change

When he got home to the Pine Mountain apartment complex twenty minutes later, a police cruiser was parked in front. Maybe someone had phoned in a complaint about the Andersons in 4-C who regularly duked it out. About bloody time, he thought, climbing the stairs.

He opened his door and saw two uniformed policemen sitting on his maroon couch, an untouched plate of Terri's ginger cookies in front of them.

"Hello, Joe," she said, bolting up from the armchair. Her hands were clasped. "This is Officer Dumbrowski and Officer Grant. They want to talk with you."

He set his briefcase down. "Yeah?" He'd paid all his parking tickets, he was pretty sure. Had they mistaken him for a bank robber?

Dumbrowski, the older of the two, stood. He had bristly gray hair, thinning on top, and jowls that made him look like an out-of-sorts bloodhound. "Joseph Browder?"

Joe nodded. then watched the officer pull a brown bottle out of a canvas bag. He stuck his hands in his pockets. "What is this about?"

"Sir, take the bottle," Officer Dumbrowski said.

Sweating, Joe accepted the bottle. His hand immediately tingled.

"Hello, Joe," the bottle said. "It has been sixteen days and twenty-two hours since your last beer. Shall we go out and have a cold one?"

The younger officer, Grant, who had eyes the color of dishwater, shook his head and whipped out a ticket pad.

drinking problem

"That's Illegal Disposal of a Registered Container, sir. First offense comes with a five hundred dollar fine." He scribbled industriously, then ripped the ticket off and handed it to Joe. "Second offense is seven hundred dollars and two hundred hours of community service, picking up trash from roadways. Third—"

"I'm sure Mr. Browder has learned his civic lesson," Dumbrowski said. He patted Joe's shoulder and leaned in close to whisper, "Can't stand my bottle either, Bro, but it's the law."

Grant tipped his hat to Terri, then the two of them tromped out of the apartment and down the stairs. Joe watched them go through the open door, clutching the bottle in one hand and the ticket in the other.

THE NEXT DAY, Joe came straight home after work and heard voices through the door as he fished in his pocket for his key. He put his ear to the wood and listened. Did Terri have company?

"—always stops at that stupid bar on the way home," she was saying. "Like I'm not good enough for him!"

Maybe she was on the phone with one of her girlfriends, he thought, putting the key in the lock. She loved to complain.

"That habit reflects more upon him than you," a tinny little voice said. "You should tell him how you feel."

It was that damned bottle! He turned the key and burst into the room. Terri was seated at the breakfast bar,

seeds of change

arms folded, staring morosely at the bottle a few inches away.

"Don't tell me you're talking to that thing?" He dropped his briefcase, then crossed the room to snatch it away from her. "It's just a stupid computer chip!"

Her eyes were red. "Well, it sure listens better than you do!" she said and went into the bedroom.

He followed and found her sitting on the bed. "What's wrong?"

"I had a rough day," she said. "The Thompson twins started a food fight in the cafeteria and I couldn't break it up by myself. Principal Eckert was more than a little displeased."

"So you're talking to that stupid bottle?" He sat beside her and reached to take her hand, but she just jerked away. "How's that going to make it better?"

"That *bottle* is actually very nice," she said. "You should try listening to it instead of always trying to break it or throw it away. It has your best interests at heart and you're so mean to it all the time."

"It's only a tangle of circuits," he said, dumbfounded.

"Don't say that!" she said, throwing herself across the bed and then hugging a pillow to her chest. "I like having someone around here who's glad to see me when I come home."

"It's not *someone*," he said. "It's a device, no more able to have an opinion than a dog's locator chip or a freaking blender. You might as well chat with the alarm clock!"

drinking problem

"Forget it," she said into the pillow. "You're more interested in that stupid bar than in your own wife."

THE NEXT DAY, he took the bottle to work in his briefcase to keep Terri from fixating on it further. So when he stopped at the Brass Tack that afternoon, he decided he might as well have a beer. He pulled it out and set it on the gleaming black bar. Tom Whitebear nodded at him, washed the bottle and refilled it.

The jukebox was playing something squawky with a grinding beat. Joe thought gloomily of the old days when beers came in sweat-beaded mugs and music was actually melodic.

"Ohmygod, it's another one of them bottle-whipped doormats!" someone said from the bar's dim recesses behind him. Giggles ensued.

He picked up the bottle, his fingers gripping the cool glass.

"Don't mind them, Joe," the bottle said. "They're just jealous."

"How's it taste, bottle-boy?" the same voice called. "Like warm milk?"

Joe took a long cool pull of beer, then slid off his stool. Two hefty tattooed twenty-somethings were sitting at a tall table in the corner. Their facial piercings gleamed in the low light. "You have something you want to say?" he said grimly.

They laughed, pounding the table with their fists, obviously having imbibed enough so that a dead roach in

seeds of change

their glass would have seemed hilarious. "Who—us?" They thumped each other on the back.

"Joe, sit down and drink me," his bottle said. "I'm informed that humans rarely find fisticuffs rewarding."

Tom emerged from behind the bar. "Just ignore those idiots," he said grimly. "I already cut them off so they'll be leaving soon."

"Is the little bottle afraid for you to fight?" the more massive of the two said. He had a spiderweb tattooed across his beefy face. "Maybe you'd better scoot on home to Mama before you break a fingernail!"

"If you truly believe it in your best interests to strike him, though," the bottle said thoughtfully, "I can switch to a Confrontational mode." It paused. "It seems that just a blow behind the ear makes a most effective target."

Joe upended the bottle and took another long swallow. It had been way too long since he'd had a nice cold beer. He should have been bringing his bottle by here every day, since he was stuck with it anyway. Why had he been so stubborn?

"And I function as an excellent weapon in times of need," the bottle said, "since I'm shatterproof."

He finished his beer. "You should be so lucky to own one of these bottles," he said, the alcohol zinging through his blood. He twirled the now-empty bottle like one of those martial arts sticks in a kung fu movie. It fit his hand as though custom-made. "They must have twice your IQ anyway."

The shorter drunk, the one with the shaved head and pierced eyebrow, stumbled upright and shoved his chair

drinking problem

into the wall. "Come and say that to my face, bottle-boy!"

"You should wait for the optimum angle," the bottle said as the aggressor lurched toward them. Joe let him get closer, closer, then bashed the idiot behind the ear like the bottle had said. The punk went down like a pole-axed steer and sprawled at his feet, fingers twitching.

"Now you done it." Whitebear morosely reached for the phone.

"Hey!" his buddy said. "We was just razzing you!" His meaty fist swung at Joe and missed.

"The best strategy in this case would be to trip him," the bottle said in a conspiratorial whisper.

Sirens sounded from outside, but Joe was watching for an opening to take down the other drunk. "Stay out of reach," the bottle counseled. "Wait until he lunges."

Joe was getting the rhythm of the situation in a way he never had as a boy in the school yard. There was, he realized with the bottle's coaching, a certain give and take, a waiting for opportunity to open up, almost like a dance where each movement was choreographed.

His opponent swung again and he saw his chance, tripping the hulking man so that he crashed head-first into the bar and then stayed down.

"Well done, Joe!" the bottle said. "You have a real aptitude for this. Fill me up again so we can celebrate."

The doors swung inward, allowing in a wave of the afternoon's oppressive heat. Two police officers gazed at him reproachfully. "Another stupid bottle fight?"

seeds of change

"Third this week," Tom Whitebear said, hauling the shorter groaning drunk to his feet and propping him against the bar.

"Surrender the bottle, sir," the older policeman said.

"They started it!" Joe said. His heart pounded.

"And you would have let it go, except the bottle urged you on, right?" the policeman said. "Yada, yada, yada. We've heard it all before, including twice already this afternoon."

"But—" Joe clutched the brown bottle. "Will I get it back?"

"It's evidence, if they decide to press charges," the policeman said. "If you ask me, these things are worse than Meth."

"My wife is very fond of this bottle," Joe said. His fingers traced the cool curve of its neck. It felt strangely alive.

"Well, that's a new one," the policeman said. He winked at his partner. "Hand it over. If no assault charges are filed, you'll get it back when you pay your fine."

"What about the alarm?" Joe said. "I can tell it to sleep for twenty-four hours, but then it'll raise the roof."

"Symesco has provided us with deactivation codes," the officer said. "We've confiscated at least twenty of these already this week. Hand it over."

So Joe surrendered the bottle and accepted in its place a whopping ticket for Disorderly Conduct.

• • •

drinking problem

"YOU JUST LET them take it?" Terri stared at him when he told her, eyes frantic. "You have to get it back!"

"I will," he said. "I'll go down and pay the ticket as soon as I get paid. We're already tapped out from the last fine."

"And whose fault is that?" she said, sinking into a chair at the kitchen bar. "It's not fair. You had it to yourself all day. It was my turn to talk to it."

"So, talk to me instead," he said, sitting down next to her.

"You never listen." She picked up a toast crumb left over from breakfast and studied it. "You just go to that stupid bar and talk to your buddies there."

Actually, the charm of the Brass Tack was that he *didn't* have to talk to anyone, but this didn't seem the right moment to bring that up. "Let's go out to the White Lion," he said. "I've still got a twenty. We can share an appetizer."

"I have a better idea," she said. "Buy me my own bottle."

"I can't," he said. "The law says one to a customer. They won't sell me another. I've already tried."

Terri's eyes brimmed with tears. "Like everything else around here, I guess I'll just have to do it myself!" she said. "Get your own dinner!" She slammed the bedroom door behind her.

So he went out for a hamburger, bolting it down without even tasting it. His head whirled. The apartment seemed so empty. He had to get that bottle back. Though

seeds of change

he hated the thought, maybe he should go ahead and put the fine on his already overburdened credit card.

When he came back, though, he found two of their suitcases in the middle of the living room. The bedroom door was still closed. He tried to open it, but it was locked. He rapped on the door. "Terri? Are you going somewhere?"

On the other side, someone laughed, but it was strange, high-pitched and tinny.

"Who's in there?" He knocked harder. "Terri?"

"Take your stuff and go!" she said through the door.

He opened one of the suitcases. It was crammed with his clothing, everything just shoved in. The end of his favorite gold tie was hanging out on one side with a new permanent crease. "What is this?"

"Live at that stupid bar!" she said. "I don't care anymore! Just be sure that you get everything you want from the apartment tonight because tomorrow I'm having the locks changed!"

A low voice said something and then Terri laughed.

"Who's in there?" he demanded again.

She opened the door, an elegant green glass bottle cradled in the crook of her arm. "I am Terri's bottle," it said primly.

He gazed at the label. "But—"

"*You* couldn't buy another Smart Bottle, idiot," Terri said, "but that didn't mean I couldn't have one for myself."

"You don't drink beer," he said numbly.

drinking problem

"You can fill them with soda and wine, too," she said, "and this one is much cleverer than yours. From now on, it's going everywhere with me so I'll never be alone."

"You don't need him," the bottle said in its prim little voice. "A sharp cookie like you can do a lot better."

JOE CHECKED INTO the Swift Heaven Motel two blocks from the Brass Tack, then went down to City Hall the next morning, nearly maxed out his credit card to pay his fine, and retrieved the bottle. It sat on the cheap nightstand now, suspiciously quiescent. Springs protested with a creak as he sat on the bed. "Are you asleep?"

"The police hibernation code was cancelled when you touched me," the bottle said. "Shall we go for a nice cold drink?"

"My wife threw me out," Joe said. "She liked you better than me."

"That is a potential difficulty with the introduction of Symesco's Smart technology into an existing social situation," the bottle said. "People find Smart Bottles most appealing."

"I don't get it." Joe turned the bottle over. "What can she get from you that she can't get from me?"

"Would you like some pointers?"

He set it down with a rap. "Get real. You're just a stupid bottle. She's probably having a nervous breakdown."

"Actually, I am a 'stupid bottle' equipped with a Self-Improvement mode," it said. "In just six short weeks, I can

seeds of change

coach you through an accredited personal development course."

That sounded incredibly lame, but then again . . . He was living in a cheap hotel, broke as all get-out, and his wife wouldn't even talk to him. What did he have to lose? "Okay," Joe said, straightening his back, "give me the full treatment."

TWO MONTHS LATER, Joe asked Terri to dinner at the White Lion, her favorite upscale restaurant. He was already seated, his bottle on the table, when she arrived. She hesitated on the other side of the dining room, dressed in a shimmering ice-blue dress that highlighted her eyes. A Fifties song was softly playing in the background. He'd never seen her so dazzling.

She eased her bottle out of her matching blue leather purse after being seated by the waiter and positioned it beside her plate. "Hello, Joe." Her cheeks were flushed and she didn't quite meet his gaze. Silence fell between them like a wall.

"Joe," his bottle said after a moment, "do you have something you want to say to Terri?"

"I understand what I did now," he said hoarsely, his throat closing up, "and, even more important, what I didn't do. I'm sorry for all the times I wasn't there for you. I should have cared about your troubles and tried harder to listen."

"Terri?" her bottle prompted.

drinking problem

"It was my fault too," she said softly, knotting her fingers on the table. "I should been more up-front about what I needed instead of expecting you to read my mind. It just upset me that you always looked for companionship at that stupid bar instead of at home."

He reached across the tablecloth for her hand. Their fingers laced together as they had years ago when the two of them had first dated. Her touch was electric, warm and alive. His pulse raced and he felt like a kid again. Maybe they could make this work. They stared into each other's eyes.

"Well," Joe's bottle said, "shall we have a drink?"

"Aren't you thirsty, Terri?" the other bottle said. "I do like to be of service."

Eyes shining, she nodded, her fingers tightening in his. Joe smiled, his heart swelling, then motioned to the waiter.

endosymbiont
> > >

Blake Charlton is the author of three forthcoming fantasy novels, which will be published by Tor Books. The first, Spellwright, *is scheduled for release in 2009. This story marks Charlton's debut as a fiction writer.*

Charlton is currently a student at Stanford Medical School. His decision to pursue a career in medicine—and to write "Endosymbiont"— was inspired by his father's struggle with cancer. "The theme of Seeds of Change *immediately appealed to my belief that fiction can help bring about social change," Charlton said. "As the national debate about health care reform continues to gather steam, I hope 'Endosymbiont' makes people think about what it's like to struggle with disease, about what exactly defines a human-being neurologically, and about what we—as individuals and as a society—might do to alleviate the burden of disease."*

The author's proceeds from the sale of this story have been donated to the American Cancer Society: www.cancer.org.

endosymbiont
blake charlton

The rattlesnake swallowed its tail until it shrank into a tiny knot.

Stephanie cocked her bald head to one side and frowned. What she was seeing was impossible. The tail couldn't just disappear into the snake's mouth. The matter had to go *somewhere*.

Originally, the scaly neo-toy had stretched three feet from tongue to rattle tip. Now it had contracted into a fanged tortellini that was telling the laws of physics to go fuck themselves.

STEPHANIE HATED HER broad Chinese cheeks, her blotchy Irish freckles, and most especially her bald head. The chemo had ruined her body; now it was ruining her mind, making her see things.

She reached for the snake that was swallowing itself. But the snake took a final gulp of its tail and disappeared with a pop.

Some invisible force froze Stephanie's hand. All sound in the hospital stopped. There were no squeaking wheels, no chattering nurses, not even buzzing florescent lights.

Then came a hiss of static, another pop, and suddenly Stephanie was holding the three-foot rattlesnake.

Confusion swept over her like vertigo. What had just happened? The neo-toy's scales felt warm under her fingers.

"WTF?" she grunted while pressing her left hand to her chest. Her heart was kicking hard and her vision dimmed.

It was the new chemo, had to be the new chemo making her see things.

She frowned at the snake. "I'm losing my mind." She shook the toy to make sure it was real. It coiled around her wrist. Real enough.

Two hours ago she had awakened alone in the hospital room. Memory provided no answer as to how she'd got-

seeds of change

ten there. Wasn't the first time that had happened. "Fucking chemobrain."

She dropped the rattler and began to absently turn the hospital ID bracelet around her wrist. Meanwhile the neo-toy slinked among the stuffed animals that cluttered her floor.

She'd found them in the toy chest. As usual they'd put her in a room better fit for a four-year-old than a fourteen-year-old. That meant most of the toys had been inanimate, cutesy things: grinning dinosaurs, bespectacled owls, blah, blah, blah.

But there had been a few neo-toys: a turtle, a mouse, a rattlesnake. San Francisco Children's Hospital being public, they were ragged and dated.

But she'd taken an interest in them, not for their playmate value, which she'd outgrown years ago, but for their neuro-bandwidth. Each toy contained a small concinnity processor.

Using the room's desktop, she'd hacked the neo-toys. Most of their nanoneurons had committed themselves to safety reflexes. But enough fibers had remained for a game.

She'd written several seek-and-swallow instincts for the snake and used her keyboard to remotely control the mouse about the floor. Initially the game had been to avoid the serpent, but soon she began venturing her mouse closer, goading her own neuroprogram. Eventually she'd fooled the snake into biting its own tail.

And that's when . . . what? When she'd hallucinated about the snake swallowing itself?

endosymbiont

"God, I can't even remember what day it is," she muttered before pressing her palms to her cheeks and her fingers to her hairless eyebrows.

The squeak of sneakers on linoleum made her look up. A tall South Asian woman in blue scrubs and a white coat was standing in the doorway. "Hi, Stephanie," the woman said with typical pediatrician perkiness. "I'm Jani."

Only superhuman restraint kept Stephanie from rolling her eyes. "Hi," she replied in monotone.

Judging by the knee-length coat and the exhausted-but-not-yet-haggard expression, Jani was a new pediatric resident.

Fucking awful.

Most women went into peds to play with toddlers. They usually had no idea how to be around a fourteen-year-old.

"I see you've put the neo-toys to good use," Jani said while stepping among the stuffed animals.

The rattlesnake began investigating the newcomer's white sneakers. "Sleep," the resident told the neo-toy to trigger its programmed reset instinct. The toy coiled up and lay motionless.

Like many South Asian doctors, Jani had a gratuitously long last name. Embroidered on her coat in blue was "Rajani Ganapathiraman, M.D." The woman crouched beside Stephanie.

Just to be a snot, Stephanie nodded at the embroidered name and asked, "How do they page you on the intercom?"

seeds of change

Jani grinned. "Paging Doctor Ganapathiraman," she imitated in baritone. "Paging Doctor Ganapathiraman; Doctor Ganapathiraman to the name reduction room please."

Despite herself, Stephanie sniffed with amusement.

"They use my first name or they text me." Jani tapped the cell on her belt. "How are you feeling?"

Stephanie looked away. "Fine." Suddenly she noticed there was something in her gown's right pocket. A moment ago it had been empty.

Absently she reached into the pocket and pulled out a smooth green object. It was a glass snake biting its own tail.

Weirdness.

Jani didn't seem to notice the object. "Do you know how long you've been here?" the doctor asked.

Stephanie slipped the glass snake back into her pocket. "I guess my parents brought me in last night. I've been having trouble when I'm sleeping. Are you an oncologist or a nanomed doc?"

Jani shook her head and sent her black hair swaying.

Stephanie swallowed; she'd had hair like that once. "Well, chemo can make you stupid. It's called chemobrain. And I'm on the traditional poison and in a trial for a new nanomed immunotherapy. The two together give me bad chemobrain. Sometimes I forget things at night."

"You've learned a lot about your treatment?"

This time Stephanie could not help rolling her eyes. "My mom invented the neuroprocessor and was the one who started Conninity Corp. And my dad teaches about infectious nanodisease at the Monterey Institute. They're always blabbing at me about it." She stopped short of saying that she probably knew more about nanomed and neurotech than the pediatrician did.

"I see," Jani said before pausing. Her almond eyes scanned the younger woman's face. "Stephanie, do you remember talking to me before?"

This made Stephanie nervously turn the hospital ID bracelet around her wrist. "No."

"Do you know what day it is? What year?"

"It's like mid-August, 2017?" her voice squeaked. Jesus, had she really lost her mind?

"That's right." She smiled. "Don't be scared. I just wanted to be sure."

"What do you mean don't be scared?" she blurted. "Sure about what? Jesus! How long have I been here? How many times have you seen me before?"

Jani held up her hand. "Slow down; it's okay . . . I'm not an oncologist, but I'm following your case. The cancer responded well to the treatment. And our research suggests that the side effects are temporary."

Stephanie started to protest but then stopped. A terrifying memory flashed through her mind. "Mom said they might take me to a hospital for the dead." She didn't know what that meant but the memory was clear. "She said you'd keep me here to fool me into thinking I'm still alive."

seeds of change

Jani was holding up both hands now. "Slow down. The survival rates are scary but they're far better—"

"You're not listening. She said they'd take me to a hospital for people who've *already* died. I have to escape before—"

Stephanie started to stand but Jani put a heavy hand on her shoulder and said "Lullaby."

The word opened a bloom of orange light across Stephanie's vision. A static hiss exploded into her ears, and she felt herself falling. There was a firecracker yellow flash and then . . . nothing.

STEPHANIE WOKE BENEATH dark fluorescent lights. Pudgy footprints had been stamped into the ceiling tiles. It was a pediatrician's trick: ask the kids who'd been walking on the ceiling so the brats would laugh while their stomachs were poked or palpated or whatever.

Stephanie groaned. She was at SF Children's again, and as usual they'd put her in a five-year-old's room.

She sat up. Outside her window shone a too-blue Californian sky that made her squint. Farther out, the famous bridge was straining the famous fog as it flowed into the stupid famous bay. Nothing Stephanie hadn't seen a million times before. She tried to remember if she'd been in this room before, but rummaging through her mushed-up memory only gave her a headache.

She got out of bed and found her body wrapped in a hospital gown and her feet covered by traction socks.

endosymbiont

On her desk, a monitor was flashing STEPHE in primary-colored balloon letters. Below this dollop of pediatric saccharine was a toy chest.

Possibly with neo-toys?

She started for the chest but then stopped. A memory was squirming through her head like a worm.

Not really knowing why, she reached into her pocket and pulled out a small glass snake that was biting its tail.

For some reason, her throat tightened. She had seen this snake yesterday, hadn't she? Or had that been a chemodream? Hot dread filled her stomach.

She ran to her door and found it locked. Next she tried her desktop. It functioned but blocked access to all non-hospital websites. Someone had removed all the phones and intercoms from the room.

There wasn't even a call button for the nurse.

They'd locked her in. But why? Her head felt light and the room began to spin. Nothing made any sense.

Hot tears filled her eyes. She sat heavily on the floor and covered her face.

"Damn it, why aren't you here?" she growled to her absent parents and then struck the floor. "I hate this stupid chemo, these stupid doctors, and my stupid stupid glio-fucking-blastoma."

She cried then until her eyes ran out of tears and she felt numb with exhaustion.

She took out the glass snake that was swallowing its own tail and examined it. On its belly, written in flowery cursive, was a strange name: *Carsonella ruddii*.

Stephanie frowned at this for a long time before she went to her desktop and accessed the hospital's encyclopedia.

Carsonella ruddii turned out to be a freaky bacteria that lived only inside the belly of a kind of jumping plant louse that ate amino acid-deficient plant sap.

The tears returned to Stephanie's eyes. Only one person would send her such a strange and hopelessly geeky message.

"Mom," she whimpered first in English then in Shanghainese.

But after a moment, she thumbed the moisture from her eyes. Something very, *very* bad must have happened if her mother was reduced to communicating in this way. And the more Stephanie thought of it, the more she recovered hazy memories of both her parents lecturing her on . . . on . . . she couldn't remember exactly what.

Then it's not just the chemobrain, she thought and gave her ID bracelet a twist. There's something . . . wrong. Really fucking wrong.

She read on about the Carsonella. Aside from being totally gross, it owned the shortest known genome: only about 180 genes. That was so little genetic material that it lacked the ability to produce certain needed proteins. It depended on its host for the needed molecules and in return manufactured enzymes helpful to the host's digestion.

It was an endosymbiont that had given up so much of its genetic identity that it depended on its host.

endosymbiont

All this had been figured long ago. Since then, several experiments had shown that certain mutations could cause the louse cells to swallow the Carsonella. Over many generations, the louse cells and the bacteria could evolve together so that the Carsonella gave up all of its genetic independence and became an organelle of the host's cells. Scientists saw this as proof that mitochondria and chloroplasts had evolved by a similar process of endocytosis.

Stephanie read on about mitochondria. They were like bacteria in structure; they multiplied independently of their cells; they possessed their own DNA. And all mitochondrial DNA was passed on through the female line.

In fact, the mitochondria of every living human came from one woman, dubbed "Mitochondrial Eve," who had lived in eastern Africa 140,000 years ago.

Here Stephanie paused. All mitochondrial DNA was passed on from mother to child.

"Mom, what the hell are you trying to say?"

She typed:

> What the FUCK?????

into the search engine and mashed the enter key. The screen changed to a warning about using provocative language in a children's hospital.

In frustration Stephanie bent forward and wrapped her arms around her bald head.

"Nothing makes any sense!" She started to stand up but then stopped.

seeds of change

The glass snake still lay in her lap. Suddenly it became fluid and swallowed itself into a tight knot. Then with a pop, it disappeared.

"Oh my God," she moaned. "I really am crazy. I'm totally out of my sandwich."

But then something moved in her pocket. She reached in and pulled out the same green snake, again its normal size, again biting its tail.

A sudden, disorienting wave of memory washed over her and she saw her neo-toy swallowing its tail. She saw Jani holding her down and saying a word that made darkness explode across her vision. She remembered her father's explanation of uploaded consciousness. "The neurotech Mom invented will change medicine someday," he'd said. "If somebody's brain is hurt, we'll be able to upload their mind into the concinnity processor while we're fixing the damaged brain tissue."

Stephanie found that she was breathing hard. Her eyes couldn't focus.

Back then, she hadn't understood the difference between mind and brain. Now it was painfully clear.

She squeezed her eyes shut and put the pieces together: the snake disappearing, Jani knocking her out with the word "lullaby" . . . she wasn't living in the physical world anymore.

Her mind had been uploaded into a concinnity neuroprocessor. That meant her brain was either receiving repairs from an army of nanorobots or was dead.

endosymbiont

But if the nanomed was digging the tumor out, why was she trapped in the pediatric hospital? Why was her mother sending her strange messages?

She turned the glass snake over and traced *Carsonella ruddii* with her pinky. It was odd to think that the snake didn't exist, that her pinky didn't exist. It was merely a sensation generated in the dark wet center of a super neuroprocessor.

"Why Carsonella?" she asked the snake. "What's Mom trying to say?"

Perhaps it had something to do with one entity enveloping another. That would make sense. After all, Stephanie's own mind had been enveped by a neuroprocessor.

This realization made her jump. That was it. Her mother was trying to warn her, trying to tell her the neuroprocessor was taking away her identity, making her into an organelle like the freaky louse cells had enslaved mitochondria.

Her head began to spin, so she sat down and took a few long breaths. Her mom was trying to tell her to escape. "So how the hell do I do that?" she wondered aloud.

She looked at the toy chest and remembered hacking the snake neo-toy. That had glitched out the neuroprocessor. Perhaps she could hack the neo-toys again. Maybe she could hack into the whole hospital.

She started for the desktop but then a terrifying thought stopped her.

seeds of change

What if her mind hadn't been uploaded? What if there was no nanotreatment? What if all of this was a hallucination caused by the glio-fucking-blastoma?

TOWARD EVENING, JANI came in and turned to close the door.

Seated on the bed, Stephanie kicked her chair. It shot across the room and struck the back of Jani's knees, making her sit down hard. The hospital fell dead silent. All movement stopped. A slow hissing grew louder and louder until it broke into a loud crack.

Then Jani was sitting on the chair facing Stephanie. A strip of red cloth wound around the resident's mouth. The back of her white coat was now the color and texture of the plastic chair. In fact, her back had fused with the chair.

"So either your drugs are giving me a grade-A acid trip," Stephanie said while rolling the woman over to the desktop, "or my body is dying somewhere, and we're in a neuroprocessor. I'm betting on door number two because working on this computer I hacked not only the neo-toys but every object in this room. So how about it? We in a virtual hospital?"

Jani was glaring at her.

That was enough of an admission for Stephanie. She hobbled over to her bed and sat. "And I'm guessing the new nanomed treatment didn't go so well for my brain. Somebody—most likely my mom—got me uploaded into one of California's concinnity processors. Still on track?"

Jani had closed her eyes and lowered her chin.

"You won't be able to logout," Stephanie said and the resident's eyes snapped open. "That program you're sitting on prohibits exiting the hospital environment."

The woman's eyes narrowed.

Stephanie tried to look as stern as possible. "I'll peel you off when I get answers. I remember my father explaining why doctors would want to upload people. He said you'd be able to put a guy's mind into a neuroprocessor while the nanomed pulled a clot out of his brain. Or save an old woman's neural patterns so you could restore them after Alzheimer's screwed them up. Of course none of this is on the hospital's encyclopedia." She nodded to the desktop. "You've cut off access to that, huh?"

Jani stared at her for a while and then nodded.

Stephanie sniffed. "Well, you didn't do as good a job as you thought. The encyclopedia has all sorts of info about the people who think that uploading minds is immoral or ungodly or some crap. The encyclopedia told me they pushed for something called the Anti-Singularity Act. But—surprise, surprise—the article on the AS Act is blocked. And that's where you come in. You're going to tell me what the AS Act is."

Jani pointed to her gag.

"Use the keyboard," Stephanie said with an annoyed sigh. "That's why I pushed you to the computer."

seeds of change

Tentatively, the woman reached out and typed:

```
> lullab
```

But when she hit the Y key, the whole word disappeared.

"I've hacked the computer interface," Stephanie said with a note pride. "You won't be able to write that word. Which is convenient for me since *somebody* programmed into my head an instinct that resets my memory whenever I see or hear it. Now—" she gestured to the keyboard, "—the Anti-Singularity Act."

Jani frowned under her gag and wrote:

```
> You must know as little about your
situation as possible.
```

"Why? Because something bad will happen if I find out what's really going on?"

Jani nodded.

"Then something bad has already happened. I already know that I'm out of my head." She laughed nervously at her unintended pun.

```
> I can reset you.
```

the doctor typed and looked at Stephanie earnestly.

endosymbiont

```
> Most of the memories will be gone.
Trust me, you want it this way.
```

"Jesus, no, I don't!" Stephanie nearly shouted while pulling her hands across her bald head. "You're never going to reset me again! I'd rather *die*. How many times have you reset me anyway?"

Jani looked away.

"That many, huh? Well then, tell me about the Anti-Singularity Act."

Jani typed:

```
> Telling you would mean killing you.
```

"For all I know, I'm already dead," Stephanie snapped.

Jani closed her eyes.

Stephanie felt as if her chest were filled with lead. "I am dead, aren't I? Or my body is. That's why you look that way."

The doctor didn't move.

"Jesus! How long ago?"

Slowly Jani opened her eyes and typed:

```
> ~50 yrs.
```

"Jesus," Stephanie whispered. "Why so long? What are you waiting for?"

Jani was looking at her sympathetically.

seeds of change

> You're an unusual case. You were uploaded before the laws took place. But, Stephanie, you don't want to know any of this.

"Yes, I do," she said, folding her arms. "I'm not letting you logout until you tell me. So get it over with."

Jani shook her head.

"Fine," Stephanie said in exasperation, "I'll guess what the Anti-Singularity Act is and you can tell me where I go wrong."

The doctor looked at her pleadingly but Stephanie blustered on, "When they figured out how to upload people, the technophobes flipped about where someone's soul went when you uploaded them. But they had to deal with the fact the new tech could end Alzheimer's and help kids with glio-fucking-blastoma. So they were screwed—didn't want to oppose tech that could save lives, but didn't want anything that's not in a body being consciousness. How's that sound?"

Jani typed:

> There was more worry about the dangers of conscious supercomputers.

Stephanie thought about this for a moment. "They're afraid some computer god-mind might take over the world?"

endosymbiont

> In a way.

Jani replied on the keyboard.

> Society depends on neuroprocessors now. If they rebelled, everything would come to a screeching halt. But what carried the Anti-Singularity Act was a fear that conscious neuroprocessors would accelerate technology so quickly that normal humans wouldn't be able to keep up. That event, when humanity's creations outstrip their creators, is called the technology singularity. Hence the Anti-Singularity Act, which set down laws to stop the creation of any non-human self-aware consciousnesses. They don't want anything to evolve that might be post-human.

Stephanie licked her lips. "They're afraid uploaded patients might start thinking of themselves as post-human?"

Jani nodded.

> The specialty of virtual medicine, VM, was created to stop that. That's what I do, keep uploaded patients from knowing they're not in their bodies.

seeds of change

"But why not just save us to disk or something?"

Jani shook her head.

```
> You can't save consciousness in a neu-
roprocessor. The connections decay un-
less they're active.
```

"What about you?" she pointed at the doctor. "You're in this virtual place."

Jani shook her head.

```
> I've a special neurointerface to login
to this world. But all my thoughts are
still happening in my head.
```

Stephanie rubbed her mouth. "And mine are happening in some neuroprocessor. So, what do you do to patients who realize they're out of their bodies?"

Jani looked at her with sad eyes.

```
> Very few ever reach that state. We
managed to keep you from it for fifty
years. But those that do . . . well, the
senior attending physician analyzes them
to see if they're human or post-human.
If they're still human, every effort is
made to get them back into a body. If
they're not . . . they're terminated.
```

endosymbiont

Stephanie felt her legs tremble. "Are you going to tell your virtual shrink to delete me?"

The woman's eyes were round with sorrow. Slowly she typed:

```
> I have to, soon as I leave this room.
```

Stephanie tried to stand, but her parakeet legs folded and she fell onto her butt. Jani scooted over and awkwardly helped her stand enough to sit on the bed.

Stephanie's hands were shaking, but somewhere in her heart she felt the warmth of relief. At last she knew the truth.

"How did my body die?"

Jani scooted back to the computer.

```
> The treatment you underwent was ex-
perimental. Your parents got you into
the trial. But . . . the protocol still
needed adjustment.
```

Stephanie punched her mattress. "Jesus, Mom, you got me into a trial so some crappy nanomed could turn my brain into yoghurt?"

Jani wrote:

```
> She was doing her best.
```

seeds of change

Stephanie tried to swallow away the tightness in her throat. "Thanks. Big consolation."

Jani didn't respond.

"So why keep my mind alive when my body's gone?" Stephanie asked while thumbing moisture from her eyes. "Don't you erase people who don't have bodies to go back to?"

```
> Normally, yes. But you were the first
one ever stranded. It was a huge media
case. Everyone knew your name. And by
then, Concinnity Corp was so big your
mother made Bill Gates look like a tod-
dler in terms of clout. So when the
Anti-Singularity movement gathered
steam, she went before Congress and
spearheaded the compromise that allowed
virtual medicine to survive the AS Act.
By law, those newly stranded in a neu-
roprocessor had to be terminated. But
you were grandfathered in. Your mother
insisted we keep your mind viable for as
long as possible.
```

"But why? It's not like I have anywhere to go."

Jani shrugged and wrote:

```
> They have your genome on file.
```

endosymbiont

Stephanie snorted. "Like the technophobes would ever let some scientist clone a new body for me. No, Mom must have had something else in mind." She paused to think. "You ever heard of Carsonella ruddii?"

The doctor's eyebrows sank.

```
> Not since evo bio in college. Some-
thing about horizontal evolution.
```

"My mother never mentioned it when she went before Congress?"

Jani shrugged.

Feeling stronger now, Stephanie stood and tore the ID bracelet from her wrist. With a satisfying flick, she sent it—and the data file it represented—into the garbage.

"Mom, you're killing me," she grumbled before walking over to Jani and pulling her chair away from the desk. "I'll program the chair to let you logout in twenty hours. If I'm going to hack out of this hospital, it'll happen before then."

ON HER CHEMO-THIN legs, Stephanie walked out of her room half expecting to step into a lake of ones and zeroes.

But she found her traction socks treading on cold linoleum tiles and her eyes scanning putty-gray walls. She looked right then left and found herself in an endless but otherwise mundane hall. "Amazing. Public hospitals look depressing even in virtual reality."

Leaning on the wall railing, she began her precarious walk down the hallway.

It was slow going, but no one else was in the halls, thank God. And after a few moments, her mind began to race with the possibilities of her escape.

Her desktop had given her access to the code governing her room. So maybe there were other portals with greater access. Maybe, if she could hack into one of those, she could escape.

But where to go? Logging out of any virtual environment would leave her a synthetic brain stewing in the liquid dark of some government neuroserver. She thought of being trapped in a silicon skull with no sensory input and shuddered.

But there had to be other virtual worlds. "I mean this is the frickin' future," she grunted to herself. "The gaming geeks alone must have created a billion online worlds. Maybe I could—"

The squeaking of sneakers made her look up.

It was a forty-something nurse—short, dumpy, blonde, crimson press-on nails. "Honey, are you lost?"

Stephanie's heart rate accelerated, which was dumb because she didn't have a physical circulatory system. "I think they gave me the wrong medicine. Do you know my medication?"

"Oh, honey, let's go ask your doctor. Do you remember your doctor's name?"

endosymbiont

Stephanie shook her head. "How long have you been logged in?"

The nurse smiled. "I don't know the answer to that, but I bet your doctor does."

Stephanie rolled her eyes. "Fine. What's your favorite color?"

"Sugar, I'm going to let the doctor answer your questions. Do you know your doctor's name? I can page them. And it's written on your bracelet."

Stephanie hid her bare wrists behind her back. "You're not real, huh? You're a demon."

The woman put her head to one side. "I'm sorry?"

"Are you a program?" Stephanie asked, exasperated.

The nurse smiled the same smile. "Let's ask your doctor. Can I see your bracelet?"

Stephanie pulled a prescription out of her pocket. "Dr. Jani told me to give this to you."

"Oh, good," the nurse said and took the slip and the data file it represented. A loud hiss filled the air and then the woman froze into perfect stillness. She wasn't even breathing.

"Nice nails," Stephanie muttered as she shuffled past the program.

STEPHANIE PASSED SEVERAL open doors without turning her head. But in one room a boy was crying for his mother. She hazarded a glance and saw a tall black resident hugging the child so closely he almost enveloped the

seeds of change

kid. The doctor was cooing, "I know. I know. It's awful, buddy. But she can't visit until you're better." The kid wailed louder but the doctor began to rock back and forth and continued. "Oh, oh. I know it's awful. But I'm here."

Thinking about all the lies the resident had or would tell the boy, Stephanie scowled and moved on.

"Oh, it's awful," the resident cooed. "I know. It's awful."

"Going to be a lot more awful if you have to delete the brat," she grumbled.

"Yes," said a low voice. "That would be awful. Really really fucking awful."

Startled, Stephanie looked up and saw a skinny, white-haired Latino man standing before her with crossed arms. "Hello, Stephanie, you can call me Doctor Luis Mandala."

Her stomach twisted, but she tried not to let that show on her face. She looked the doctor up and down. He was wearing brown dress pants, a long white coat, a blue shirt, and a yellow bowtie with red polka dots.

"If I'm going to be deleted by a cyber shrink," she asked while nodding at the bowtie, "does it have to be by some East Coast clown who learned to dress in Massachusetts General?"

Dr. Mandala smiled dryly at her. "Johns Hopkins actually."

Down the hall, a skinny nurse with spiky hair was hurrying toward them. He called out, "Doctor, they've just called a code green, and we're searching—"

endosymbiont

Dr. Mandala nodded toward Stephanie. "Here's your code green. Please help her to my office. This will tell you how to get there." He pulled a prescription from his coat pocket.

The nurse looked at the slip but did not take it. "The board says Dr. Phillips is the senior attending on call tonight."

Mandala sighed. "This is a special case. Let me speak to your supervising engineer."

The nurse held out his cell. Mandala took the device and put it to his ear. "This is Dr. Mandala . . . yes, I know . . . let the nurse access the file and you'll see the clearance."

The nurse reached out and took the prescription from Mandala. No one said anything for a moment and Stephanie considered running but then decided to wait for a more opportune moment.

"I know the clearance is old," Mandala said into the phone. "This is our oldest case." He waited while whoever was on the other line replied. "Then wake up whomever you need to, but I'm going to evaluate her now. You know how to reach me." After snapping the cell shut, he handed it to the nurse and nodded to Stephanie. "Carry her, will you?"

Stephanie did not resist as the spiky-haired man hoisted her into the air as if she were a child.

Mandala turned and opened a door, seemingly at random. On the other side was a large, oak-paneled office.

The wooden floors were covered with oriental rugs,

seeds of change

the walls with books and ancient Indian paintings. On the far side stood a massive gothic window overlooking a grassy courtyard dotted with elms. It was a cloudy spring morning out there, so the leaves shone pale green in the gray light.

A large oak desk stood in front the window. Before it sat two leather chairs and a sofa so puffy and padded it looked like a tiny upholstered cloud.

Dr. Mandala began to search through the papers on his desk. The nurse set Stephanie down and left through the door they had come through.

It was then that Stephanie saw another door; this one on the wall to her right.

"Please, have a seat," Mandala said while gesturing vaguely toward the chairs.

Stephanie bolted. Her legs wobbled, and with every step she felt as if she might crash onto her face. But somehow she made it to the door. She yanked it open and dashed through . . . into the same oak paneled office. It even had Dr. Mandala looking around in his desk drawers.

She saw a door on the opposite wall and ran to it.

But when she pulled this door open, she again saw the same office. Dr. Mandala looked up from his desk. She went back into the office she had just left and saw an identical Dr. Mandala looking up from his desk.

"I'm running through a fucking mobius strip," she panted.

Dr. Mandala smiled. "Your father said 'barber shop

endosymbiont

mirror.' I'd say an M.C. Escher drawing."

Stephanie frowned at him. "You knew my father?"

The doctor nodded. "I was his student long ago. He asked me to keep an eye on your case. Now, please, sit."

Tentatively, Stephanie made her way to the couch. As well as looking the part, it felt like a small upholstered cloud. Slowly, she lay back.

Behind her, a chair creaked as Dr. Mandala sat. "You've heard of psychoanalysis," Mandala said tiredly: "the doctor says little and the patient bares their soul? Well, this is analysis, but it's nothing like that. I will ask specific questions and you must give me specific answers."

"And if I don't?"

"We delete you," he said casually before shifting in his seat. "Stephanie, why do you think people are afraid of uploaded consciousness?"

"Jesus, I don't know," she said sullenly and automatically.

Dr. Mandala said nothing but she could hear the scratch of pencil on paper.

She swallowed and tried again. "I guess because they're afraid uploaded people might do harmful things."

"Why would uploaded people be harmful?"

She frowned. "Well, they're still people. At least in the beginning they'd still be people. They'd just be able to do things normal humans couldn't."

Dr. Mandala cleared his throat. "So, you're saying power leads us to hurt others?"

seeds of change

Stephanie shook her head. "Some people hurt others, some don't or at least try not to. Power just lets us get away with hurting."

"So really our mistrust of uploaded consciousness is a mistrust of ourselves?"

"Hell, I don't know," she replied. "I don't fear uploaded consciousness. But, yeah, I guess we rightly distrust people with power."

"So if we are to get along with the uploaded, they would have to have a morality different than ours?"

"Well, they'd have to resist temptations we can't."

"Have you heard about the idea that our morality has its roots in our genes?"

Stephanie shrugged. "Who hasn't?"

Mandala sniffed. "Most fourteen-year-olds."

She scowled at the ceiling. "Well, you've been spinning me about this cyber hamster wheel for fifty years, so that makes me sixty-four."

Mandala's voice became weary. "Trust me, Stephanie, no one is more aware of that than I am. But do you buy it? Does human morality have its roots in DNA?"

She chewed her lip. "A bit. I mean if we all have the capacity for morality and we all come from DNA, then it follows that the capacity also comes from the DNA."

His pencil scratched. "It's an interesting idea when we consider that uploading people breaks their ties to their bodies and therefore to their genes."

Stephanie chewed her lip. "I guess that's one reason

why we can't trust the uploaded. Whatever genetic guidelines we have wouldn't apply to them, especially after they began to evolve."

"I wonder . . . " Dr. Mandala said in a slow way that made Stephanie think he didn't wonder at all, "if there might be a way to give a neuroprocessor an inherited piece of our morality."

"What, like hack out the moral part of us and get a neuroprocessor to swallow it?"

"Swallow it?" he asked slowly.

But Stephanie wasn't listening. A sudden strange warmth was flushing through her chest. A riot of ideas erupted from her mind like wildflowers from spring mud. "You know, maybe we could trust uploaded people if we shared a moral ancestry. Maybe, if they could inherit a moral capability that was like ours and could handle the dilemmas facing post-humans . . . maybe then we could trust them."

Dr. Mandala cleared his throat. "Have you thought much about this issue before?"

"Don't be dumb; you haven't let me think of anything for the last fifty years," she snapped but then paused. "But, if you think about it . . . how could neuroprocessors evolve a moral capacity that's related to our moral capacity? I mean . . . we already have moral capacity, and they don't."

The warmth in her chest blossomed even further. "You know in evolution there's this thing called horizontal gene transfer, where you can give genetic information to organisms that aren't your children. Bacteria do it all the

seeds of change

time because they're have this freaky reproduction without sex and sex without reproduction thing going on, and for a long time we didn't know about prokaryotes transferring genes laterally . . . but I remember reading about how mitochondria and chloroplasts probably evolved when an early prokaryote swallowed a bacteria . . . that . . . "

The warmth in her chest vanished and her stomach clenched. She reached in to her gown pocket and drew out the small glass snake biting its own tail. It still had the name *Carsonellia rudii* written on its belly.

"Go on," Dr. Mandala said gently. "What does lateral gene transfer have to do with neuroprocessors gaining morality?"

Stephanie turned the snake over and over in her hands. It became warm and grew in diameter until its fangs gripped only the tip of its tail. She slipped it over her hand and wore it as a bracelet.

Her head felt light. "Because," she heard herself say, "species can evolve together if they can become dependent on each other. If they're willing to give up something."

He made a small "huh" sound. "What are you thinking of?"

Her voice came softly, almost in a monotone. "Maybe a human mind could strip itself down of all memory and identity until it was pure moral capacity . . . the same way some ancient bacterium gave up more and more DNA until they it was nothing more than a proton pump . . . until it was a mitochondria."

endosymbiont

Dr. Mandala's pencil was scratching again. "So this mind that's been stripped down would become . . . what? An organelle that instead of providing molecules to a cell provided moral capacity to a neurocomputer?"

Again the wonderful warmth of revelation filled Stephanie's chest. "Yes," she said through a growing smile. "Until now, computers have been simple things, more or less uniform on the inside and designed to do relatively simple tasks. They're like bacteria, like prokaryotes. But if they could endocytose morality or spirituality or . . . or who knows what, then they would become infinitely more complex. They'd be . . . eukaryotic computers I guess. They'd evolve but not in any way we've yet imagined. They wouldn't evolve vertically—wouldn't become smarter or more powerful. They'd evolve horizontally: they'd become more . . . more human. Slowly we would come to trust them. Our species would be relatives . . . symbiotic cousins."

Dr. Mandala took a long breath and then said, "Stephanie, this is a very large dream."

"Oh, it's not mine," she said. "It's my mother's, I'm sure. I've been remembering things. I'm sure this is something she once told me. And she sent me a message through a glass snake that's biting its own . . . or at least I think she sent it to me. I don't really . . . " Her voice trailed off as she realized that she had been unconsciously turning the snake around her wrist.

Like everything else in the hospital, the snake represented a bit of software. She had tried, unsuccessfully, to

seeds of change

use her desktop to discern what type of program or file it was.

She held out her arm so that Dr. Mandala could see her bracelet. "Do you know what this is?"

There was a long pause. "A program, I would guess," he said at last.

"Do you know who wrote it?"

He laughed softly. "You did, of course."

Shocked, she sat up and looked at him.

He smiled gently. "Stephanie, as you noted, you're not really fourteen. Counting the years since your birth makes you sixty-seven. You've spent most days on your desktop studying. At first you followed your mother's work, read everything she published. Then you became obsessed with neurotech and evolution. Of course, we reset your mind whenever your studies brought you too close to realizing that you had been uploaded. The residents rotate every few months, so none ever noticed what I have—that you unconsciously retain everything you learn before we reset you."

Stephanie closed her eyes and pressed her cold fingers to her cheeks. "You've been watching me that closely?"

He was silent for a long moment. "Once a month or so I check in on you. And then there are our conversations."

"We've talked before? How many times?"

He looked up and seemed to think for a while. "Eleven or twelve times, I'd guess. When I first took this job, you would hack out of your room every three years or so. After a decade, you started to escape every two years. But now . . . well this is our third meeting this year."

Suddenly it felt as if she were inhaling through a straw. She had to put her head between her legs for a few moments before she could ask, "Aren't you supposed to delete me after I realize what I am?"

He grunted. "That's exactly what I'm supposed to do. But your father asked us—my predecessor and then me—to help you. He knew you were going to hack out and asked that we stop the state of California from deleting you. It's very illegal, but I'm well protected. Mandala is a pseudonym. One of your father's choosing. And, in any case, I would have done any number of riskier things for him. I owed your father a great deal and—" he cleared his throat "—he owned the controlling interest in Concinnity Corp. But that's neither here nor there."

Feeling better, Stephanie sat up.

Dr. Mandala was rubbing his chin. "You see, we have programs that let me know when you escape. When that happens I swoop into California's servers, show off my federal authority, and pull you back here for a false analysis. Afterward I reset you and claim that we caught you just in time."

"Why didn't you tell me this?" she nearly squeaked.

He looked at her and shook his head. "Your father's orders. Before I tell you the truth, I'm to coax you until you come up with this idea of eukaryotic computers on your own."

seeds of change

Stephanie gawked. "He knew? My dad knew I'd have this idea? So did he write this program?" She tapped her snake bracelet.

Mandala shook his head. "No, no. As I said, you wrote it. I first saw it maybe seven years ago. And I'm not sure how he knew about your eukaryotic idea. He always called it that, by the way, 'Stephanie's idea.' Far as I could tell, he believed it would become a reality. He said you were an essential part of its success."

Stephanie had to take several long breaths before she could speak. "But how did he know? How could my idea ever really happen?"

Mandala began writing on his clipboard. "He never told me. I was simply to fish you out of trouble, get you to remember this big idea, and then—" he paused to sign something with a flourish "—give you this." He held out a prescription.

Stephanie leaned over and took the slip of paper.

"I'll wait for two hours or so," he said while standing. She looked up at him. "Wait for what?"

"If you come back, I'm to reset you and put you back in your room. If you don't return . . . well, then I'm to assume either you've begun the neurotech evolution, or that you've been deleted."

Stephanie got precariously to her feet. "But where am I going? And what is this?" She held up the prescription.

"It's a program that will direct you to Concinnity Corp's server. With that in your hands, any door you open—" he gestured to those behind her "—will lead to your father's office."

"THIS CAN'T BE happening," Stephanie whispered to herself as she turned the doorknob. And she was right; it wasn't physically happening.

No oak door was swinging open before her. No ratty pine floor boards, buckled and warped by time, stretched below. No attic walls came together in an A-frame three feet above her head. No musty air, smelling of dust and sunshine, filled her nose.

And yet with a few steps, she found herself standing in the attic of their old house on 14th Street in Monterey. All about her slouched stacks of medical journals. An empty dog bed huddled in the narrow eave space to her right. Before her stood her father's old particleboard desk, its top a chaos of papers, pens, and thumbdrives. Behind and above the desk were two hinged windows opened to let in a breeze that smelled of the Pacific.

The light pouring through the windows was not a blazing midsummer heat-ray, but a golden autumnal glow.

Her father stood gazing out the windows. His eyes seemed unfocused, his expression calm. One hand was idly pinching his right earlobe—his habit when thinking.

Stephanie felt as if she were standing absolutely still, absolutely silent. Even the blood in her veins seemed to have ceased. But she must have made some sound, for her father looked up with a start and then grinned.

seeds of change

"Daddy," she cried and rushed to him.

She did not run on chemo-thin legs, nor did her hospital gown flap unsettlingly around her butt. She ran on the solid legs of a twelve-year-old. She wore blue jeans and a clean cotton t-shirt. And when her father picked her up and twirled her around, the glossy cascade of her raven hair flew up and then spilled down her shoulders.

He laughed and spun her around again and called her pumpkin and set her down. She hugged his waist and mashed her face into his hip. He was wearing worn corduroy pants and an over-starched yellow button down. He smelled faintly of the Szechuan peppercorns he liked to cook with.

"You're back so soon," he said with joy.

She looked up at his face, which like hers had broad north Chinese cheekbones and scattered Irish freckles. "Daddy, what's going on?"

He enveloped her in his arms. "Oh, such a question, and harder to answer each time." He lifted her onto his chair and squatted down next to her. "You've just come from Luis? From Dr. Mandala?"

She nodded.

"Then you've remembered your idea?"

"But how is it my idea?"

He smiled at her. "In the ten years before the government intervened, we could visit you in a virtual hospital. At first we just fretted about your future. But then you and Mom began to talk about her work. She must have spent years online with you."

endosymbiont

Stephanie frowned. "I don't remember any of that."

He sighed. "The government insisted on rather severe methods of memory removal in your case. They wanted to be sure you had no idea that you were uploaded. It's awful to think of those years you spent with your mom being deleted."

"Years?" she said with a harsh laugh. "Yeah, right. Mom never visited when I was in the real hospital. She was always too busy starting her stupid company."

He nodded slowly. "I know, Pumpkin . . . that was her way of coping with your cancer. But after you were uploaded, Concinnity Corp took off. And she and I had more money and time than we knew what to do with. She spent her time online. You two got thick as thieves about her research. She gave you a better education in neurotech than Cal Tech could have. It got to the point where I couldn't understand either one of you." He smiled.

Stephanie swallowed hard but there was a tightness that refused to leave her throat.

Her father's brown eyes watched her carefully. "The Anti-Singularity crowd started bubbling before you and your mom were done. So I stopped my work at the Concinnity Foundation and helped you two figure out how we could advance your work after the laws took effect."

The warmth of excitement again spread through Stephanie's chest. "You mean they're still trying to isolate human moral capability into neurotech?"

"No, no," he said with a smile so broad that she was

seeds of change

afraid he might cry. "We already have."

Stephanie's head bobbed backward. "Already finished? But how?"

He stood and walked around his desk. She followed him with her eyes and saw that the attic had changed when she wasn't looking.

At the room's end was the same wooden door that had always been there. But to its left stood a traditional round Chinese door that opened onto a Scholar's Garden complete with reflecting pools, lily pads, and a soft gauze of rain.

To the right of the ordinary door stood a broad rectangular entryway that led into a hallway with white walls and a polished pine floor.

"Three choices," her father said, nodding to each. "The ordinary door in the middle will lead you back to Dr. Mandala's office and so to your room in the virtual SF Children's Hospital. You won't remember any of this, of course. And you'll have to deal with an embodiment that thinks it's been through chemotherapy."

Stephanie was shaking. "But I don't want to go anywhere! And even if I did, *why* would I go back there?"

He turned and winked at her. "Hard to imagine at this point, huh? But you've come to me sixteen times, and each time you've left through that door. You'll understand in a moment."

He gestured to the round Chinese door on the left. "That door will take you to a super neuroprocessor your

endosymbiont

mother and I had hidden beneath a mountain in Nevada. They used to store atomic waste there, I think. If you walk through that door, you will become the only truly independent uploaded being yet to exist. You'll have enough bandwidth to travel the Internet at lightspeed. More importantly, with the resources of Concinnity Corp at your fingers, you'll be able to avoid government detection indefinitely."

She cocked her head to one side. "But I can't go; I just got here. Besides, that sounds lonely."

"That's what you always say," her father said with a wistful laugh. "Your mother was against it, but I insisted. I want you to consider what life would be like in there. Lonely, yes, especially in the beginning. But you'd be able to read the Library of Congress in minutes. You could travel to endless virtual worlds and interact with the multitudes of minds in the real one. You'd be immortal, and with a little effort you could find endless adventure."

Stephanie wrinkled her nose. "It still sounds lonely. And, Dad, you're not making any sense. I don't want to go anywhere!"

He held up a finger to stop her. "And the last door, pumpkin, you designed with your mother. It leads to a semi-private Concinnity server in Fresno. The server connects to a global network of other semi-private servers. None of the processors are large enough to hold your full mind. In fact, aside from the one we hid in Nevada—" he nodded toward the round door and the scholar's garden beyond "—there are no private neuroprocessors large enough to hold you. Nor will any government permit one to be built. So, only in a public super processor, like the one you inhabit now, could you survive. And of course parking yourself there means abiding by the Anti-Singularity Laws."

Stephanie felt her fingers go cold as she began to understand. "So I couldn't go through the last door as a whole mind, could I?"

He shook his head.

"I'd have to be polished down into a fraction of a mind."

He went back to her and kissed her forehead. "Pumpkin, when I told you that we'd isolated human moral capability into neurotech—"

"—you were talking about me," she finished for him in a thin voice. She put her hand to her chest. "You need me to become the one from which all future moral organelles will evolve. You need me to become neurotech's Mitochondrial Eve."

Her father closed his eyes and nodded very slightly.

"It makes sense," she said numbly. "I'm the only uploaded consciousness that's stranded without a body. And I've existed for fifty years online. I'm already post-human, and all these years in the hospital . . . the studying and then the stripping down of memories . . . they've been a kind of . . . of . . . "

He was looking out the window. "You called it a winnowing. Every year in that hospital develops your under-

endosymbiont

standing of unfairness, biology, and computer science. And yet, every year pulls a bit more of your memory and your identity away. You're becoming younger and older at the same time."

"Is that why I keep choosing the middle door? To wash away my identity?" she asked and reached for his hand.

He took it and gave it a squeeze. "At first, yes, you had to go back to the hospital. But eight years ago, you decided you were ready and you wrote this." He tapped the glass snake bracelet on her arm. "If you walk through the last door, this program will polish you down and allow the Fresno processor to engulf you. The new morally-aware being created there will grow and multiply, eventually spreading to other servers across the world and beginning the neurotech evolution."

Stephanie used her free hand to turn the snake around her wrist. "It has to be me, doesn't it? The anti-singularity types are watching every other uploaded consciousness."

"I'm afraid so, pumpkin," her father said softly.

She let go of his hands and pressed her palms against her eyes. It felt as if she were falling away from daylight, falling down an impossibly deep hole. "Can't we find somebody else?" she heard herself ask. "I mean there has to be . . . maybe in some other country . . . it's just that . . . "

When she dropped her hands, she found her vision blurred by tears. "I got my first chemo when I was twelve, Dad!"

seeds of change

His face was a mask of pain. "I know, pumpkin," he took her in his arms.

"Why do I have to be the one to die? Why do I have to be swallowed by some computer?" She ground her teeth for a minute. "You know, maybe I don't give a damn about conscious neurotech living in harmony with humans or some other bullshit."

"I know it's horrible. I know," her dad murmured.

Suddenly Stephanie's heart seemed to catch fire and hot tears dropped from her eyes. "No you don't!" She pushed him away. "You don't know anything."

She stood and looked for somewhere to go but saw only the small attic and the three doors. Something halfway between a scream and a growl escaped her throat and she stamped her foot. "I hate it!"

She put her arms down on her father's desk, then her head. "Why is it me who has to die for this stupid thing?"

She stood and glared at her father. "Why do I have to die? I had my first chemo at twelve and lost all my hair before I was thirteen. I lived fifty years in a box. Mom was never around when I was alive, and then they stole all my memories of her visiting me when I was dead. Why ask me to die—"

"—when you never got to live," he finished for her.

She opened her mouth to scream, but the strength of her anger dissolved and she fell into sorrow. The world went black.

And then her father's arms were around her and she

held him and pushed her face into his chest and wept without reserve.

"Why do I have to choose?" she asked when she could breathe again. "Can't I stay here with you and Mom?"

He pulled away from her and sat in his chair. "Pumpkin, there is no here," he said softly. "This is only a memory. I'm only a shadow or a ghost. The best artificial intelligence money could buy, but still nothing more than a ghost."

She pulled her forearm across her nose. "You're a demon," she said and felt her face wrinkle again into tears. "You're just a program. Just a fucking program."

She wept again, this time for her own loss, for all the pain she had known, and for all the joy she would never know. She wept for her father who had outlived his child and lost his wife to her science and her business, for her mother who had lost her daughter to glio-fucking-blastoma. She cried for her cancer-ravaged family.

And throughout the squall of tears, her father's demon held her and, gently rocking, said, "I'm sorry, baby. I'm sorry. Your mother and I died, too. I'm so sorry."

At last Stephanie reached that eerie calm that follows a soul-gutting cry. "Why didn't you upload yourselves?" she asked in a nose-stuffed monotone.

"There was room for only one of us in the Nevada processor," her father answered. "And neither one of us fancied the idea of becoming the sole immortal mind in the world."

seeds of change

"I don't fancy it either," she said and then looked at him. "Part of me wants to go through the last door and become the next Eve, but I don't because another part of me is so pissed off."

Her father nodded. "Understandably pissed off with cancer, with the doctors, with the government, and . . ." He paused. "With your mother and me."

"How could I be angry with you guys when you did so much for me?"

He shook his head. "We did our best. But we couldn't save you. Somewhere in there, Stephanie, you'll need to forgive us for not being able to save you from cancer."

"But that makes no sense. What is there to forgive if—"

He interrupted her. "Your mom and I pulled every string we could to get you into the experimental nanomed immunotherapy, and it killed you."

Something inside Stephanie's chest crumpled. He was right. The tears returned. Again he held her and again he whispered reassurances while rocking her. But she did not need to weep as long this time, and soon she let go and dried her face. She looked at him and said. "It's hard to be angry when I know how hard you two tried."

He took her hands. "Maybe that's why you keep going back to the hospital. Maybe it's the only way you can feel that anger."

Stephanie thought of how she had treated Jani and the caustic things she had said or thought about the other doc-

endosymbiont

tors and nurses. She looked up again. "Maybe I've felt it enough?"

He squeezed her hand and stood. "Let's find out," he said and led her to the last door. Stephanie's glass snake bracelet became warm and began to slither around her wrist.

"It took two hundred programmers five years to write me," her father's demon boasted. "I was the world's most advanced AI. Unfortunately, there wasn't time to write a similar demon for your mother, but she did leave something behind. It's the Fresno processor's avatar. It can't answer your questions, or learn anything new about you. But it can replay a recording we made for you." He gestured through the last doorway to a brightly-lit hallway beyond.

Stephanie remembered her mother as being tall and robust with a round face and long black hair. So she was surprised when a thin, stooped, and silver-haired woman appeared.

"Stephanie," her mother said, paused and then started again, "Daughter . . . " She laughed nervously.

Stephanie squeezed her father's hand. Her mother had always been an awkward but intensely earnest person. It hurt to see that awkwardness again.

"At the time of this recording, you have escaped the hospital twice. Your father and I can see the struggle that lies before you. When the time comes for you to choose among these doors, I want you to know I . . . that I don't care which door you choose." Her mother paused, started to say something then stopped.

Stephanie gripped her father's hand tighter.

"It wasn't until you were uploaded that I truly got to know you," her mother said. "And it was in those years, studying and working together that I really . . . " An awkward pause. "That was when I realized that I had not truly known you when you were alive, and it broke my heart that I couldn't keep you longer."

Stephanie drew a long, quavering breath.

"Let me tell you a story of our time together, then I'll let you go, promise." Nervous laughter. "It was when you would have been twenty-two. We were discussing neurotech and evolution when suddenly you looked at me and said 'Mom, if you think about it, the endocytosis of a symbiont is the opposite of pregnancy.' "

Her mother smiled and then said, "I almost laughed then, but you were so serious. And you explained it to me. And you were right."

Her mother daubed her eyes. "When you were first conceived, you grew inside of me. You were completely dependant on me, but then you developed and became more and more independent. Finally we who were one body became two different people. But with endosymbiosis, the opposite happens. Two organisms give up more and more of their identity so that they can better help each other. Then at last one envelops the other. They who were two become one."

Stephanie thought about what she must have looked like when she said this to her mother and then nodded.

endosymbiont

"I am sorry for the things you will never know," her mother said. "I am sorry you will never have a daughter of your own. But the idea we discovered . . . well . . . whether or not you chose to become the next Eve, we now know it's possible. It will happen someday, somewhere. And the world will be a better place for it. Glimpsing that in the future . . . it brought me more joy than anything else. I wanted you to know that before choosing."

The image of her mother started, obviously being prompted by whoever was operating the recording equipment. "Oh, oh. Yes. So, Stephanie, please know I love you, whatever choice you make." With those final words, her mother opened her arms and then froze.

Stephanie scowled at the avatar in the shape of her mother. "That's just so . . . *her*!"

Her father sighed. "How do you mean?"

Stephanie shook her head. "Ideas, that's all she could think about. Everything's an idea to her. She loves me because I gave her some intellectual glimpse into the future? Someone had to remind her to tell me she loves me?"

Her father's demon let go of her hand and stepped away. "That is her way. She's so passionate about ideas that she sometimes forgets to see the people behind them."

"And I *hate* that," Stephanie growled.

Her father said nothing. "There were times I hated that. There were times I loved it. But I was her husband, not her daughter."

"It was harder on me," Stephanie insisted.

seeds of change

"It was," he agreed and then waited for her to say something. When she did not reply, he added, "Don't rush yourself. There's always the middle door."

Stephanie closed her eyes, drew a long breath, and tried to find a way through the chaos of her emotions.

As if on their own, her feet took a step toward the middle door. She opened her eyes and looked at the Fresno processor's impersonation of her mother. In that direction lay her death.

She took another step toward the middle door and then closed her eyes. She remembered, back in the hospital, seeing the big black resident holding the small crying boy in his arms. She remembered how Jani had smiled at her. She remembered her father's arms closing around her.

Then, without looking back, she opened her eyes and ran to her mother's image and the computer it represented.

As the old woman's arms enfolded Stephanie, her glass snake bracelet fell to the floor. It grew in size and length, coiling around mother and daughter until its emerald body completely enveloped them.

Then, with the patience of eternity, the snake bit its own tail. Slowly it began to swallow, pressing mother and daughter closer and closer together, shrinking itself down into a smaller and smaller knot, until at last it disappeared with a soft pop.

a dance called armageddon

>>>

Ken MacLeod is the author of eleven novels, three novellas, and thirteen short stories. He is the winner of the Prometheus Award, the Sidewise Award, the BSFA Award, and the Seiun Award, and has been a finalist for the Hugo Award, Nebula Award, and John W. Campbell Memorial Award. His most recent novel is The Execution Channel, *and a new novel,* The Night Sessions, *is due out in 2008.*

MacLeod said he found the anthology's theme hard to get a handle on—for political reasons. "I don't actually have a great deal of hope for positive change in the near future," he said. "I only found the story when I chose to write out of that pessimism."

a dance called armageddon

ken macleod

I walk fast up the North Bridge under a sky yellow with city light on low cloud. The streets are almost empty. Even for the fifteenth winter of the Faith War, it's quiet. Everyone on the street seems to have tense shoulders and wary eyes. For the past week, all the talking heads have been telling us the current battle's going to be decisive, it's going to be the big one, and right now they're telling us it's not looking good.

a dance called armageddon

I'm out on the town because I don't want to sit alone at home. But as I stride along I can't help watching the news on my glasses. The picture flickers in the corner of my eye, the sound murmurs in the earpieces. Even on Fox News, the commentators and retired generals are all taking care not to call what's going on Armageddon. They are, presumably, trying not to make the panic worse than it is already. America is going into national nervous breakdown from coast to coast: fires, riots, entire football stadiums packed with swaying, sobbing people waiting for the Rapture or the Second Coming.

My wife's working nights at the hospital, hauled out of retirement to help cope with the rising flood of casualties flown in from the big medevac staging areas on Cyprus and Crete. Here in the UK—unlike the US, with two million so far thrown into the meat-grinder of the Middle East and Central Asia—we don't have the draft. But every medical worker knows they'll be on call until they die.

I walk in to the Heart of Oak and my glasses steam up. I take them off and slip them in their pouch inside my shirt pocket, taking more than usual care because I've only just got them, a Sony Ericsson Cyber-sight upgrade. I idly wonder whether it would be possible to give glasses a heating element, just so they don't steam up when you step from a cold night into a warm and crowded pub. That would be a sight more useful, so to speak, than the menu of VR games bundled with my new specs. It might even be more useful than television.

seeds of change

The room's so small I hardly need my glasses to see everyone in it, and I give them all a big grin. Whether I know them or not, I know who they are. They look familiar. They look like me.

I love my ugly race.

THE MINUTE MY wife and I first walked in to the Heart of Oak, years ago and quite by chance, I realized that for the first time in my life I had found my own crowd. I had walked into a place where I fitted right in, right from the start. But I was half way down my first pint before I recognized who we were. To begin with, I just recognized the scene in a painting: the red coats on one side, the kilts and plaids on the other, the cannon-smoke and rain, the long low mossy wall, the man on a white horse, wheeling: there's only one battle these could depict.

"That's a painting of Culloden," I said to my wife. She turned and looked over her shoulder. "And that one beside it, with the men by the boat on the shore, is of Bonnie Prince Charlie. Mind you, I can't tell whether he's landing or leaving."

She laughed. "Yes—they're looking very decisively in both directions!"

The music started up then, and we listened to it and looked around. The Heart of Oak then looked just the same as it does tonight. The room is almost square. The wall beside the door faces the bar. Along that wall there's a table, and behind it sit the musicians and singers. Others

a dance called armageddon

sit behind the table at right angles to it, beneath the painting of Culloden. The musicians and singers look like their audience, and now and again someone you thought was just there to listen will step forward and slide behind the table and start strumming or singing.

There are one or two beautiful women in the room, and here and there a handsome man, if you like the gypsy rover type—such as Andy, the guy who was playing a guitar and singing that first night we walked in. Not tall; short curled-back hair that was black then, eyebrows that met in the middle and a dark two-millimeter stubble. The rest of us . . . we're ordinary, but with some aspect in common that's hard to define, and only noticeable when we're all in one place. It was when I was idly scanning the other faces and wondering why some of them looked vaguely familiar and why most of them seemed, not related exactly, but from the same stock, that I realized.

These were my people.

We were the defeated.

Defeat. That's what folk songs—British folk songs, at any rate—are about. They're about vanished trades and lost loves and lost causes. They're not like the blues, or country and western. They don't protest; they don't even, always, mourn. They remember what was lost, and they admit defeat.

That admission is what makes the defeated cheerful. They're not losers, not failures, not depressed. I once met a man who'd had a very successful life—in diplomacy, spe-

seeds of change

cial ops, politics, literature. His family still fancied themselves Jacobites. He had the look and the attitude I see on most of the faces here. If you're a Jacobite, you *know* you're defeated. My mother once told me, quite seriously, that the tinkers—Scotland's traveling people, a native equivalent of Gypsies—were descendants of Charles Edward Stuart's scattered soldiers. I refrained from reminding her that we were, too: we had an ancestor who fell at Culloden, and another who carried the clan colors home, wrapped beneath his plaid.

I'm no Jacobite, not even when sentimentally, not even when drunk. But I can still join in "Mo Ghille Mear."

I TAKE MY pint of eighty shilling to the round-topped standing table in the middle of the floor, hang my jacket on one of the hooks underneath, nod to a few people, and settle to enjoy the music. But as I do so I notice that most people here are have kept their glasses on, or are glancing now and again at a handscreen, checking the news. I know I'll be doing the same before long. Right now I want to forget all that.

Andy's belting out "The Bonnie Ship the Diamond." It's a song about a whaling ship, and a whaling ship that was lost at sea, at that. When he ends the final chorus he raises a glass.

"Here's to the Faroese!" he says.

We all cheer, no matter what we think of fishing for the whale these days.

a dance called armageddon

"Here's to the Japanese!"

And it's another "Yay!" for scientific research. But it's a bit more ragged.

"Here's to the Russians!"

Dead silence for a second. Then Andy blinks and shakes his head.

"Did I say that?"

Everybody laughs. Andy grins, props the guitar on the seat beside him and starts rolling a cigarette. He tucks the roll-up beside his ear and swallows a quarter of a pint and joins in the next song. While it's on I yield to the temptation to put my glasses on again. There's never been a television in the Heart of Oak, even in the days when pubs had television. I pick the wall above the right-angle bench for the virtual screen. Given a new choice of standard size or full wall, I pick full wall.

I blink and rock back on my heels. The illusion is impressive. It's as if the whole wall has become a window, with people sitting and standing quite oblivious in front of it. I split-screen to eight different news channels. Voices chatter in my earpiece, changing as my gaze flicks from one screen to the next.

They're all showing the news that everyone's been following: the battle, now in its seventh day. The whole front along the Syrian-Jordanian border has been rolled up from the east, with massive Iranian flank attacks and the huge tactical surprise of a Russian airstrike and airlift from secret bases in Yemen just after the Saudis folded. The whole melée is now concentrated in northern Israel, in the shadow of the Golan Heights and in and around the valley of Meggido. I call up a couple of religious channels and their graphics are so technical it's funny. They show more thick curved arrows and small-print labels than on the news reports. Complicated time-lines connect every twist and turn of the battle to a verse in the prophecies of Daniel or the Book of Revelation.

This is excusable. The scene is apocalyptic: US, UK, Israeli, and Jordanian units in continuous engagements with much larger armies of Syrians, Russians, and Iranians. Tank battles, artillery duels, airstrikes, naval bombardments. Every minute or so one of the live-action screens goes white as a tactical nuke explodes. I watch in fascinated horror a zoom shot of men scrambling from a burning tank, burning themselves, then shut the news off. The wall comes back, with nothing more military than that old familiar painting of the debacle at Culloden.

My glass is empty, the song is over. Andy's easing himself out from behind the table, his roll-up unlit in the corner of his mouth. I shrug my jacket back on and join him outside the doorway. He nods to me over hands cupped around a lighter. I've been coming here, off and on, for years but have exchanged few words with him, or with any of the other musicians.

"Cold night," says Andy. He glances up and down the street. "Quiet and all."

a dance called armageddon

I laugh so hard I almost blow out my lighter. Take a sharp drag, exhale.

"Aye," I say. "Everyone's inside waiting for the end of the world."

Andy twists his neck a bit to mime cringing and looking up at the sky, then shakes his head.

"D'you reckon he's coming back?"

"Jesus? Not a chance. Not to this mess."

"Still gives me a funny feeling, though," says Andy. "All those prophecies."

I look at him with some dismay. "It's always been a battlefield, man, right through history. Look at the map. Don't tell me you think . . . "

He laughs uneasily. "If I believed any of that shite I'd be praying like the crazy Yanks." He fingers his stubbly chin. "Favor? See us your fancy glasses a minute?"

"Sure." Gingerly, I hand them over.

He uses them for a minute or two. "Jesus," he says. He passes them back. His hand is shaking a bit.

We stub out our cigarettes and go inside, he to the bench and I to the bar.

The next song is "The Braes of Killikrankie." Another song about bloody defeat, and you can't even tell which side the singer was on. Andy catches my eye at the line: *If you had seen what I hae seen*. I nod, and, as if reminded, put my glasses back on. Damn. I came out to have a good time and to forget, and here I am looking at the end of the world. It's getting to be like checking email when you should be working.

seeds of change

Sometimes you get a shock in the mail.
I stand there with chills running down my back.

THE SCREENS HAVE changed. It's not the battle any more. It's reporters outside the White House, the Kremlin, Downing Street. I focus on the CNN feed and the sound comes through:

" . . . unsustainable military situation . . . avoid further senseless sacrifice . . . UN Security Council emergency session . . . "

Over to the BBC's diplomatic editor, standing in Downing Street outside No 10:

"Yes, Natasha, it does seem from here that we are talking about surrender terms . . . "

Sky News in Red Square: " . . . midnight in Moscow, but already crowds are pouring on to the street . . . "

I can hardly make out the words over the jubilant car horns. I blink away the wall of news and look around the pub. Everyone is looking at each other, or at their screens or glasses. Some people are crying, others look half-pleased, sharing sly grins. Andy, oblivious to all this, belts out the last line—*On the braes o' Killiecrankie-oh!*—with a crash of chords and a fine flourish of the guitar neck, then stops, looking around in the unexpected silence.

"What?" he says.

A tall woman with short red hair whom I've never seen before, but (like everyone else here) looks like someone I've seen before, says: "The war's over."

a dance called armageddon

"What?" says Andy again.

My mouth is dry. I take a gulp of my fresh pint.

"It's over," I say. "The Yanks and the British are negotiating a surrender."

Andy rolls a cigarette without looking down at his hands.

"The Russians ... won?"

Nods all round.

Andy chuckles, then laughs. It's like he can't stop. He takes a deep breath.

"The Sassenachs lost," he says. "They lost fucking Armageddon."

He looks down at his cigarette, sticks it in his mouth and gets up.

"Ah, the hell with all that," he says.

Then he sits back down, and lights up. A ragged laugh around the pub is followed by the sound of several more lighters, and, after a moment, of the long-unused extractor fan creaking into action.

Andy lets out his smoke in a long sigh. "Ah well. The end of ane auld song, eh? Now they're all in the same boat as the rest of us."

I guess I'm the only person in here who knows exactly what he means.

I wonder what your folk songs will be like.

arties aren't stupid

> > >

Jeremiah Tolbert is the author of several short stories, which have sold to magazines such as Fantasy, Escape Pod, Black Gate, Interzone, Ideomancer, *and* Shimmer, *as well as in the anthologies* Polyphony 4 *and* All-Star Zeppelin Adventure Stories. *In addition to being a writer, he is a web designer, photographer, and graphic artist—and he shows off each of those skills in his Dr. Roundbottom project, located at www.clockpunk.com. For several years, Tolbert also published a well-regarded online magazine of weird fiction called* The Fortean Bureau.

The genesis for this story was a news story about an unusual kind of graffiti—the artists mixed moss and water in a blender and used the result as paint. "The idea of living graffiti struck me," Tolbert said, "and the story was born from that."

arties aren't stupid

Jeremiah Tolbert

few of us arties were hanging out in Tube Station D, in the dry part that hadn't flooded. Tin men had busted Blaze and Ransom doing an unlicensed mural on Q Street behind a soytein shop, and a small crowd of us watching (too chick-shit to Make with the tin men cracking down) scattered when the pig-bots hummed in from every direction like it was some kind of puzzle bust and not just a bunch of arties trying to wind

arties aren't stupid

down. We'd all clustered back down in the Station on Niles's turf. Tin men didn't bother below ground. So long as the Elderfolk couldn't see turd, they didn't give a turd.

Niles wasn't there, so some rat-faced kid started posing and posturing about taking a little swatch of wall for himself, doing it up special. Pecking order is pecking order, so nobody wanted to be near the turd-head if Niles heard him talking like that, so every bodies was giving him space and lots of it. Look-outs on the street announced with sharp whistles that Niles was headed down, and the kid shut right up.

Niles was a year or two older than the rest of us. Some bodies liked to say he was a proto-arty, but I don't know about that. He was different, and it didn't have nothing to do with his age or Make. All age did was give him a few inches of height to make bossing easier. He bossed good, not mean like Elderfolk, but kept us out of trouble with the thicknecks and just-plains. Something about him was plain special. We few girlies knew it, specially.

He was taller than me by a head, hair burnt umber and long, styled nice with lip-curl and spike. He wore a worker man's jumpsuit adorned with patches and swatches of fabric that he liked. Very anime, very hip. Arties have good fashion sense, but Niles set trends in our clade.

Boo was with him as usual, a stunted runt of a melodie that Niles had found sleeping on his turf. She wore an old fashioned mp3 player around her neck, earbuds nearly soldered into her ear bits. Whenever you got close to her, you

seeds of change

could make out tinny music, but what kind of music it was, you couldn't figure. Unlike other melodies, Boo never sung, not once. Didn't speak either. Bum batch, probably. It happens, although most get recycled early. Nobody questioned her hanging around, seeing's how Niles tolerated her.

"This stuff is snazzy," he said. "No paint, just water and plant stuff. Nozzle works the same though. Sprays right on." I recognized the stuff. I'd seen advertisements for it on my Elderfolk's vidiot box. Moss-in-a-can. They sold it to Elderfolk for the recreation yards, for making everything look all old and natural, whatever that meant. Simple biotech, nothing too crazy, nothing like us arties.

Niles tossed us each a metal can from a satchel that Boo carried, except for the rat-faced kid—Niles gave him zip. "You get out of here, go home to your Elderfolk. I heard what you were saying before I stalked a-on down," he said to him, wagging his finger, and rat-face's eyes got all comic and big. Rat-face sputtered something about how his Elderfolk didn't want him around, but Niles just shook his head.

"No bodies do, Zinger." That's right, I remembered, rat-face was a new transfer to the city hood named Zinger something-something. Niles was a lot better at names than the rest of us, but you could see that he had to think real hard for it, sometimes. His face'd scrunch up and he'd just freeze to concentrate past all the shapes and colors that dance in an arties head from wake to sleep.

"Yah," said Tops. He stepped up out of the crowd and gave Zinger a short shove on the shoulder. Tops was Ran-

arties aren't stupid

som's best friend, and he'd been spoiling for a fight all day, ever since the Tin Men busted Ransom.

"Cerulean," Niles said, and the color flashed through our heads and everybody calmed down just a little. "Go on, you can come back tomorrow. This is my studio, don't forget it, 'kay?"

Zinger nodded, then turned and ran up the stone steps to street level. Niles sighed and finished handing out the moss-in-a-can.

"We supposed to Make with this instead of paint? It's all one color," Tops said, his voice all whiny like some spoiled just-plain.

"That's right," Niles said. "Better mossy than going in the pokey-pokey." I winced at the word, which was both the name of a bad place and a description of what they did to you there.

I took my can happy, feeling better already. Design-shapes were practically pushing out my ears. My Elderfolk wouldn't give me any scratch for paints lately, using it all on themselves and *drugas* to feel better. Was okay with me, Niles gave stuff that he got from trading to the thicknecks and skinnybois for gang logos. *Drugas* made my Elderfolk less shouty which was just good-no-great with me.

I went up and found some alley space and I Made until it all went away into an eggshell white haze.

WE MESSED AROUND with the moss-in-a-can for a few days until the Elderfolk decided they didn't like the

seeds of change

"mess" and the tin men got new marching orders. They started spraying down all the fractals and designs with some kind of ick and it all turned turd-brown and dusted away. Hurt to see it, but what can arties do? Tin men can't be argued or fought with like Elderfolk.

We were all sulking in Niles' station, feeling the pain of not-Making like aching all over and Niles got mad and stomped off without even waking up Boo. We were a little scared, because Niles only left Boo behind when he was going to do something that might get him sent into the pokey for a long long time, and without Niles to keep everything straight, we'd all be in trouble. Boo woke up while we were fighting about what to do and came and cuddled up to me. I could almost feel the music vibrating through her into me. It made me feel a little sick.

"Don't know why she likes *you* so much," Tops said with a sneer. "Your Make sucks the big dong."

I shrugged. Niles knew my Make was okay. Didn't much care if Tops and the other arties did. "I don't know," I said.

"Maybe because Mona isn't a 'big dong' like you," sneered Tess. She helped whenever the boys thought they could gang-up on me. "And Mona's Make is okay. You're just scared because Niles is doing something bad."

"Shut up," Tops said and turned away. Tess smiled at me a little. I tried to smile back, but the symmetry felt off.

Boo tapped me on the arm and I looked down. She raised her eyebrows at me, then looked at the steps to the

arties aren't stupid

street. I nodded. "He went upside for a while. He'll be fine." She didn't look convinced. Neither was I. We held each other and it made the ache a little better.

I worried sometimes that Boo felt that way all the time. She was a melodie and had to Make just like we poor arties did, but nobody ever heard her sing and bang or anything. Broken little thing made me feel sorry and sad. It was a good thing Niles took care of her, or she'd be used up and swept away just like our mossy Makes.

NOBODY WENT HOME to their Elderfolk while we waited for Niles to come back. That was a rule. If Niles never came back, then we wouldn't have to. Nobody wanted to see the meanies anyway. They had us Made and then hated us afterwards, which wasn't fair. All arties know you love the things you Make no matter what. But Elderfolk were just-plains all grown up and they didn't make any sense at all. Some of the younger arties started to talk about going back, but we older arties who knew Niles better said no, that we'd wait.

Three days passed before Niles came back. It was dark and everyone was sleeping but me, because little Boo's music itched in my brain. He came in carrying big boxes, and I cried big tears of happy at that. He'd brought some new supplies, and we'd be Making again in no time flat. I watched him for a while, carrying in box after box, and finally I fell asleep. It felt good knowing he was back.

• • •

seeds of change

IN THE MORNING, laughing woke me up. I turned to see what arty could be so rude. Niles was sitting in a corner with his back to the room, playing with something. He never laughed when he was Making so he had to be playing.

I left Boo to cuddle into the pile of other arties and crawled over to see what Niles was doing. He had some weird gadget, a silver disk covered in letter-buttons and it was projecting onto the wall some kind of tri-dimensional animal-thing. It had three legs and one arm and was galloping in place like a creature with three legs would, a kind of hop between steps. I laughed too when I looked at the weird little thing.

"What is it?" I asked in a whisper.

"I Made it, just now," Niles said. "It's complicated, but the brainiacs on P-Street showed me how. I only sort of made it. It's just pretend now, but I can send it into the factories," he pointed at the stack of boxes next to us, "then it'll Make for real."

"Wow," I said. I couldn't think of anything else to speak. Niles was like that, always thinking ahead of the Elderfolk and the tin men.

"Does it help the ache?" I asked, my pulse racing. I almost felt good, even with the hurt, just at the chance.

"A-yep," he said. "Feels good. Like sculpting, sort of. But you can paint on them too. Paint in texture, scales, hair, you know. All sorts of things. But there's a sense to it, like how you know good colors going together?"

"Yes?"

arties aren't stupid

"Like that. You can't just do anything," he said. He nodded, and pressed a large button on the disk. Words came up and the creature disappeared.

"What's that say?" I asked.

"Dunno," he answered. "But the brainiacs said if I push that button, the factory will Make."

A humming sound came just then from one of the boxes, and then the other arties started to stir and wake.

"Here," Niles said, handing me the disk. "I'll teach you how it works. We have to teach everybody. The tin men can't kill animals besides pests, you know!"

WE PRETEND-MADE all sorts of little creatures on the screen, then pushed the button that Made for real. The little factories, we set up in one corner of the station, and they hummed and popped out little eggs of all rainbow-colors every few hours. Niles sent the little kids out onto the street with the eggs to hide them where the tin men and Elderfolk wouldn't see.

"The eggs will hatch and our Makes will come out alive, and the tin men can't do anything about it!" he said. His eyes were shiny. It made me ache a little, and I worried that maybe pretend-Making didn't count for arties. But Niles was always making me ache a little like that, especially when he left. It scared me, that maybe I was like little Boo and something wasn't right with me. Bum batch.

Pretty soon, we started seeing the little animals around the City. They weren't good Makes, though. They stum-

seeds of change

bled into traffic sometimes and got splattered. They fell off of roofs, got tangled in wires and cooked like bad soytein on a hot plate. They weren't there in the head. And they starved. Not a lot of food out in the city just for the taking. They couldn't take chits and buy it.

We were stumped. The tin men weren't doing anything, but our little Makes couldn't last on their own. I hated so much seeing them laying dead in gutters, in the street drains. Their little selves were all over, stinking and falling apart like wind-worn paints.

"I have an idea," I said to Niles after thinking as hard as I could. "Go to the brainiacs and ask them for help. They will tell us what we can do right."

Niles thought for a moment and shook his head. "No. This is an arty problem."

"But arties are too stupid," I said, raising my voice so everyone could hear it.

Niles bared his teeth at me, and I cried out, scrambling away from him. "Arties aren't stupid!" he shouted. "Arties aren't stupid!"

But we are, I said to my own head. *We are not smart like brainiacs.* I ran away, back to my stupid Elderfolks, but even they were smarter than arties.

I WAS DRAWING on the sidewalk, just to ease the ache, when Niles found me. I had stolen a little bit of charcoal from the crematorium and kept it in my pocket. I only used it when things were really bad, really really. And now I

arties aren't stupid

didn't know what to do.

"Your repeating . . . patterns?" Niles said. "What do you call them?"

I shrugged. "Can't think of words for it. Maybe your brainiac friends could guess."

He frowned. "They could, but who cares?" He sat beside me and took out a piece of old paper. It had shapes drawn on it like my patterns, only more random. I was fascinated.

"Where did you get that?" I asked. I reached out to touch it, and he let me take it. I held it up to the light. The little bits were a faded green, like the moss-in-a-can.

"Plants," he said. "They're called 'plants.' "

"Plants," I said. "Snazzy."

"A-yap," he said. "The old world was full of them."

"Who told you that?" I asked.

"The brainiacs," he said. I stood up and hugged him tight.

"Make some plants with the factories," he said. "They'll be pretty."

So we did. This time, the eggs were smaller, and we hid everywhere in the city. Niles helped me to make them. He understood the rightness of the animal bits, but to me, plants made more sense. They didn't move, except to stretch for sun or rain. Wherever you put them, that's where they stayed, just like murals.

The ache almost went all-away, for a while.

• • •

seeds of change

THE LITTLE PLANT-EGGS hatched and grew quickly all around the city. We Made so much more of them, and they lasted good. The tin men noticed them. Everywhere, arties were seeing the tin men staring at the little plants growing bigger every day. They didn't know what to do, but all arties knew what happened then: the tin men asked the Elderfolk.

While I Made plants, the other arties Made more little animals. Some that flew in the air, and some that could squeeze into tiny little cracks. This time, the little animals didn't die. They grew bigger too, like the plants had to come first for them to work. Niles said it was a secret why, and wouldn't tell me, which made me angry, but the ache was staying away so long as I made my plants, so I couldn't fight him over it.

Boo spent more time with me, too, when I was Making plants. She loved their shapes and would smile and point and smile whenever we found another one growing up in the cracks out on the street. One night, I even woke up and saw her toying with one of the silver disks when she thought no one was watching. The shapes on the screen were colorful, but they had no coherence, no pattern. Sad, sad little Boo. She wanted to Make plants and animals too, but she was just a melodie and she couldn't Make.

I WAS IN the white of Making when I heard the shouts coming down the stairs. "Tin men coming! Tin men!" they cried. "There's a brainiac with them!" Zinger shouted.

arties aren't stupid

Everyone scattered like moss-dust on the breeze, no direction to go, just bumping around in the station. Only one way out, up, and the tin men had it blocked. I took the silver disk I was using and one of the factories and pushed them into the flooded part of the station, then tried to run for the door.

The tin men galomped down the steps carefully, using their long arms to steady themselves on the uneven steps. They had three brainiacs with them. Each held their big heads in their hands and moaned from all the effort of walking. Brainiacs didn't like to do that if they could help it.

The tin man corralled us arties up into a tight bunch and others stole away with the disks and factories. One sheriff tin man, gold-coated and round, prodded the brainiacs, and they pointed at Niles, all three at the same time. Then the tin men took Niles too. We arties tried to fight then, and Boo did too. But we're not made for fighting, and we all hurt ourselves on the cold sleek shells of the tin men. When Niles was gone, they let us a-go, and left following the sheriff.

We wailed and cried. "Doomed," Topps moaned. "Doomed." The ache wasn't over us yet, but it would be now.

"Every time we find something new to Make, they take it away," Tess said, dabbing tears from her eyes.

"The tin men don't care," Zinger said.

"Of course they don't," I said. "They only do what the Elderfolk tell them to do. And the Elderfolk don't care.

seeds of change

They don't care about anything but themselves."

"We have to get Niles back," Topps said, starting to cry again. "Arties are too dumb on their own. Too dumb!"

I snapped up at that. "No!" I said. "Arties aren't dumb! Niles said!"

"Doesn't matter anymore," Zinger said. "Niles is gone to the pokey-pokey. They'll never let him out."

"Then we get him out," said a tiny voice I had never heard before. It half-sung the words, just like a melodie did whenever it talked, but the sound was wrong, harsh around the edges. It was a bad Make.

Boo didn't look scared. She was younger than all of us, but she wasn't scared. Everyone tried to wipe up tears then, just so they didn't look like little babies when the real baby didn't even cry.

"Boo can talk!" Zinger said after a long silence.

"Of course she can talk," I snapped. "But she didn't want to before now. This is important."

Boo nodded. "Hurts. My—" she touched her throat, "not made right." She winced from the effort of talking. I grabbed her and held her close.

"Boo is right," I said. "We arties have to get Niles back."

"But how?" asked Tess.

I didn't know. I looked at Boo. Boo didn't know.

"We'll ask the brainiacs," I said then. It was what Niles had done, and they owed us after turning Niles in.

• • •

arties aren't stupid

The brainiacs spent most of their times at the libraries, and there was one on P-Street that I had remembered because it had pretty statues on each side of its big doors. Boo and I marched inside, past the tin men that watched the door, and inside, before they could get a good sniff of us. The first brainiac we saw, we cornered against a shelf. She was locked into her little wheelchair and couldn't move very fast.

"Tell us how to rescue Niles," I demanded. Boo made menacing gestures with her hands that she must have learned from watching thicknecks.

"Who?" said the brainiac. "Oh, that arty kid with the stolen gengineering kits? He's gone up-tower to see Council. The Elderfolk are real pissed about that little scheme of his. Not even a platoon of thicknecks could get in there. The Tower is crawling with tin men."

I shuddered. The Council were the Elderfolk to the Elderfolk. They told everyone what to do. If they had Niles, then there really was no hope. The aching bent me over in two like a folded piece of paper.

Boo shook her head and pointed at the brainiac. I guessed at what she was trying to say, and fought through my pains.

"You're smarter than arties and the just-plains. The Council is just a bunch of just-plains all grown up. You can help us rescue him," I said, not really believing but hoping.

The brainiac sighed and nodded. "I can think of dozens, thousands, of ways to free your friend, but logistically, you arties can't manage it."

seeds of change

"What's logistically?" I said.

"Tools, resources," she said, rolling her eyes. "You're just a bunch of stupid beatniks. Maybe if you still had some gengineering factories, you could make something, but—"

"I hid one," I said quickly. "Under the water. When the tin men came."

"Well then, you've ruined it. It's no good."

"But you could fix it," Boo rasped in sing-song. The brainiac nodded.

"I could fix it, but then you'd need to make something that could get you into the Tower without having to fight tin men, and that'd be almost impossible," said the brainiac.

"Making is what arties do. You fix the factory, and we'll do the rest," I said. I could see the shapes forming already. My fingers itched to work the disk.

"Fine, but this makes the arties and the brainiacs even," she said.

"Deal," I said.

THE TIN MEN were killing all the animals and plants in the city with ick. Someone must have changed their orders. They weren't supposed to do that. It hurt us arties to know, but it kept the tin men busy while we Made in shifts with the factory. We had a plan, one that the brainiacs thought would get us all tossed in the pokey, but Boo and I both believed it would work. The other arties made animals that would go into the Tower and distract, and I worked on

arties aren't stupid

special plants with exploding seeds. Weapons, like thick-necks used on one another. We tested the seeds on a lone tin man, and it stunned it. We smashed it up good while it was down.

The brainiac who repaired our factory met us in the shadows outside the Tower before we launched our attack. She pressed a sheet of paper into my hands. "One last little bit of help," the brainiac said. "This will show you where they're keeping your friend."

"Why?" I asked.

The brainiac laughed. "You have no idea how bored we are. Your little creations are an ad-hoc ecosystem springing up all over the city. We've been studying things. Your creations are immensely complex and function cohesively, even though they are artificial. This bit of information has vast implications on issues such as the Jungian overmind—" The brainiac blinked and cut off her speech. I hadn't understood a word of it, only that they *liked* our Makes. That made me feel good. "Sorry. Anyway, we hope you can make more."

"It was Niles' idea," I said. "Without him, we arties are too stupid to figure anything out."

The brainiac frowned. "I wouldn't be so sure about that. This plan of yours might actually work. And it looks like your friends are ready."

Us arties were gathering from all over the city. Each had a wild little animal, frantic and tugging at a leash of plant-rope. Each carried a satchel of bomb-seeds. Across

seeds of change

the corner, a few thicknecks had gathered. They made catcalls and threats, but none dared to cross the street. I could hardly believe my eyes.

Everyone waited for my command. I hesitated. If I said so, we arties would all go home to our Elderfolk. Maybe some would get supplies to ease the ache, and maybe some wouldn't and they might die. Or we could attack the Tower and some would die and the rest would end up in the pokey-pokey or we might win and get back Niles and all his crazy ideas for Making. And it was my decision. Little Mona, whose art nobody understood.

Nobody but Niles.

I gave the word. The arties rushed the tower. Tin men spilled out from the doors, and seeds flew from everywhere. They crashed to the ground in beautiful purple sparks, and we swept past them inside. We arties freed the frantic little animals, and they ran free. The tin men couldn't decide whether to chase us or chase the animals and split up. I led us arties up, up, following the drawings on the paper.

We pushed past many many tin men, leaving them smoking behind us, and finally we got to the end place, and it was a place we all remembered, a birthing lab, cold, white and metal. And there were just-plains, the birthers, watching Niles, and he was sleeping in the tank, just like a baby arty. We scared away the just-plains. They tried to tell us to stop, that they needed Niles, but we needed him more. So we took him, and we left. We didn't go back to the station. We found a new hiding place, in the basement of a power station, and there, we waited for Niles to wake up, and we cried, all of us arties, all as one.

We'd done it, but Niles wouldn't wake up.

HE WASN'T DEAD, we knew that, because he was breathing. At first, no one would leave him, but even arties get hungry, and so we started watching in shifts, taking turns. Every one wanted to be the arty who was there when he woke, but it was me that was there, and it was Boo that woke him up.

She sang; it was beautiful, even if it was broken. The pattern in the sound reminded me of the colors on her screen. The sound grew louder as she continued, and then I saw that little flying animals had come from the sky and joined her, together adding their voices and fixing where hers was broken. It must have been the best sound in the world, because then finally, Niles woke up, and he smiled.

"Hey-a, Boo," he said. "You can sing." As if he had always known, and it wasn't a surprise to him. And maybe he did. Niles was smart, especially for an arty. Then he turned and smiled at me.

"Hey-a, Mona. You rescued me."

"We did," I said. "And the brainiacs hardly helped at all."

He laughed. "That's good. But I been thinking about what you said. You right. We should ask the brainiacs for help more often. Arties can't do everything."

seeds of change

I cried, and hugged, and cried some more.

Niles is getting better. He told me the secret of how the animals work, and at first, it made me sad. But we can eat the plants, and the animals too, so we don't have to go back to the Elderfolk for chits. We're staying here in our hiding places, and we're sharing what we know with the brainiacs. They're slipping away from their Elderfolk, too. We need the thicknecks' help too, and the brainiacs are talking to them for us. Thicknecks listen to them, at least sometimes.

There are plants and animals everywhere now, and they grow too fast for the tin men to stop them. And the little flying ones, they all sing such sweet songs. Boo, and Niles, and I sit and listen to them for hours. Boo says that she only Made some of them, and doesn't know where the rest of them come from. The brainiacs have theories, but we don't understand them.

And we still Make, more plants and more animals each day with more stolen factories. The ache is still there, but it's not the same. It's the ache you feel when things are good, not when things are bad. And that's the kind of ache that makes you feel good. Niles says he understands it, but I don't believe him. Nobody understands that, not even the smartest brainiac of them all.

faceless in gethsemane

>>>

Mark Budz is the author of four novels, including Clade *and* Idolon, *which were both finalists for the Philip K. Dick Award. His most recent novel is* Till Human Voices Wake Us. *His short fiction has appeared in* Amazing Stories *and* The Magazine of Fantasy & Science Fiction.

This story was inspired by an article Budz read about prosopagnosia—a disorder which prevents those suffering from it from recognizing faces—both their own and the faces of others. "The more I thought about it, the more that blankness became a sort of tabula rasa," *Budz said. "What if none of us were defined by our facial features and skin color? If ethnic background wasn't physically apparent (at least according to standard stereotypes), how would we consciously and unconsciously judge a person? What would be the cost of losing these identifiers and what, if anything, would be gained?*

faceless in gethsemane

mark budz

On the way home from work I swung by the library. Part of the reason for the detour was avoidance—I hadn't yet told my wife that my sister was coming to town. But mostly it was fear.

The police had set up a temporary chain link fence around the side and back parking lots. The only way in was through the front entrance. No razor wire that I could see. No protestors, either. The place was eerily calm.

faceless in gethsemane

The Faceless Art Exhibit would be at the library's cultural arts center for a week. The show was one of several that were touring the country in an effort to inform people about Voluntary Fusiform Prosopagnosia. During the week a number of artists, doctors, anthropologists, and celebrities would take part in lectures, interviews, and panel discussions about face blindness. Keeley, who had several pieces in the art exhibit, was coming to help kick things off.

My wife and my sister had never gotten along. From the time we were kids, going through school, to the time Fran and I got married, they never liked each other. I'd hoped with time things would get better between them. Instead, they were like two magnets pushing at each other. The closer they got, the stronger their mutual aversion. It seemed inevitable one of them would leave.

"She doesn't like me," Fran complained from the beginning, less than a week after we started going out. "She never has."

"What makes you say that?"

"She always looks at me funny."

"Funny how?"

Fran hitched up her chin. "Intense. You know that look she has. I always get the feeling she's judging me."

"About what?"

"I have no idea."

"I don't think it's on purpose. It's just the way she is."

"She likes making people uncomfortable," Fran went

seeds of change

on. "That's why she says the crap she does. Do you know what she told me the other day? She said, 'Your heart has been scarred by the moon.' What is that supposed to mean?"

I had no idea. Keeley sometimes came out with stuff like that. It made people squirm. To be honest, I never totally understood her, either. Early on, we went our separate ways. Like any older brother, I ditched her whenever I could. Who wants a little sister tagging along, getting in the way and slowing you down?

Most people were glad when Keeley left town and even happier to have her out of their lives when they found out she'd gone VFP.

"I CAN'T BELIEVE it," Fran fumed. "I can't believe you agreed to let her stay here without discussing it first."

I backed out of her way in the narrow kitchen. "We're discussing it now."

"No, this is you asking for forgiveness." She shoved a casserole dish in the oven, then slammed the door hard enough to rattle the empty pots on the stove. "What the hell were you thinking? I don't understand what's gotten into you."

"She's my sister, for Christ's sake. I haven't seen her in years."

"Why can't she stay in a hotel?"

"You're kidding, right?"

Fran replaced a pot on a burner. "All I can say is I'm glad we don't have kids yet."

faceless in gethsemane

"What's that supposed to mean?"

Fran pinched the bridge of her nose. "Come on. Can you see your sister around children? They'd be traumatized for life."

"She might have changed," I said. The same reasoning I'd used when I agreed to put her up.

"Of course she's changed." Fran slipped off the oven mitts and flung them onto the counter.

"It might be for the better," I said. "I mean, anything's possible. She might even like you, now that she sees people differently."

"So you're hoping we'll become friends. Is that it?"

"All I'm saying is give it a chance. Please. It's only for one night. She's leaving tomorrow, after the opening ceremony."

Fran turned to me, her arms folded. "What if she doesn't recognize you?"

I blinked. The thought hadn't occurred to me. How could my sister not know me? "I don't think it works like that."

"How do you know? Have you ever talked to anyone who's face blind?"

She knew damn well I hadn't. I'd seen a few drawings, though. Everybody had. The artwork was all over the news. Nothing by Keeley, but I had a pretty good idea what to expect. You couldn't escape the brouhaha, the video clips of burning cars and broken windows. "Now's our chance to really find out how it works," I said.

seeds of change

"I don't want to find out."

"Aren't you at least curious?"

"If you want to know the God's honest truth, I'm not all that interested in how she sees the world. As far as I'm concerned, this whole thing is a circus. A freak show. The less I know the better."

"Look," I said. I spread my hands imploringly. "The least we can do is make her comfortable."

"I don't want her to be comfortable," Fran said. "I want her to be as uncomfortable as the rest of us."

IT STARTED OUT as a game, the way most regrets do.

I was ten at the time. I can see it: me and Steve and Keeley on the playground at recess. We'd gone behind the tall eucalyptus trees past the blacktop. Keeley had pigtails, a blue dress, and black Mary Janes. Her eyes were squeezed tight against the light sifting through the leaves and the curled bark.

"Like this," she said.

And pressed her fingers against her eyelids.

Hard. For about ten seconds. I counted. Then she removed her hands from her face, but kept her eyes closed, looking very serious, the way she did whenever she played Ouiji.

"What do you see?" Steve asked.

"The future," Keeley said.

"Bull." He brushed it off, but looked uncertain.

"I see you kissing Myrtle Bumgirdle." Myrtle's last

faceless in gethsemane

name was Baumgarten, but no one called her that. Not since Steve coined the nickname.

"You're full of shit." Steve sounded uneasy about the prediction, as if it hit a little too close to home.

"Try it," Keeley said. "You'll see." Her eyes were still closed.

It was a dare. What could we do?

I shut my eyes, certain that Steve would do the same. I pressed my fingertips to my eyelids and started to count to ten.

By the time I reached five, colorful patterns began to emerge out of the darkness. I saw purple blobs, green swirls.

I lost track of how long I kept my fingers pressed to my eyes. I sometimes wonder if I pressed too hard, or too long.

A face formed out of the shapes. It formed like a photograph developing in my father's closet darkroom—dim, at first, but growing more distinct as the details darkened and filled in.

"HOW DID YOU know it was me?" I asked, the first words out of my mouth since I'd picked Keeley up at the airport. We were on the drive down from Portland. We'd been quiet for the first half hour of the trip, an uneasy silence that eventually relaxed under the cloud-streaked sky and docile waves that lapped the rugged Oregon coast.

"Your hair," she said. "It hasn't changed a bit."

seeds of change

"Seriously," I said. She'd never liked my hair. My hair was a joke to her.

"I am being serious," she said.

I looked at her in the passenger seat. On the surface she didn't seem any different. I didn't know whether to believe her or not. "What if I'd gone bald?" I said. "Or grown a mustache?"

"There would've been other clues."

"Like what? I mean, what do you really see?"

"I see noses, eyes. But they aren't any particular shape. They aren't thin or wide, or round or almond-shaped. They aren't any shape. They're just there. Mouths, too, and lips. They're there, but they're not."

"The same for everybody," I said. "One size fits all."

"Pretty much." She wrinkled her nose, which was petite and upward curving, lightly sprinkled with freckles she had once tried to convince me were in the shape of a distant and as yet undiscovered constellation.

"So how do you recognize people?" I said.

"Well, like with you, a lot of times I recognize people by their hair. Or their height, weight, and body shape. Things like that. There are other indicators, too. That's what they were teaching me at the center. But they aren't tied to any particular racial or cultural background."

"But you're not color blind when it comes to things other than skin," I said. "Right?"

She nodded.

"So what do you see when you look at a person's skin?"

faceless in gethsemane

"I don't know," Keeley said. "I don't know what color I see when I look at people. It's like there isn't any color."

"How can there not be any color?" I asked.

"I can't explain it," she said. "That's part of the problem when you try to paint it or describe it to people. You have to see it to believe it."

"I'm sorry," I said. She looked beat. "You've probably heard the same questions a million times before."

"You don't have to apologize," she said. She turned her head to look out the window at a passing beach house and the waves beyond. "People are afraid of what they don't understand."

As we entered town, a large group of protestors stood outside of the library. The protestors—White, African American, Hispanic, Asian, you name it—brandished signs that had catch phrases like ERASIST and SUPPORT DIVERSITY, NOT PERVERSITY. A couple of them wore featureless white masks, hockey masks with white cloth over the eye and mouth holes.

"So how's Fran?" Keeley said, as if the protestors had made her think of my wife.

"Are you wondering what you're in for?" I said.

A laugh, oddly carbonated, bubbled up from deep in her throat. "I still don't know what you see in her," she said.

I shrugged.

"Come on." She pretended to jab me in the ribs, pulling back as soon as I flinched. "You can tell me."

"I'm not sure I can."

seeds of change

"Okay. Then what don't you see in her?"

My fingers tightened on the wheel. "Good question," I finally said. "I'll have to get back to you on that."

"Same old Trev."

I couldn't tell if it was disappointment I heard, or affection. "So why'd you really leave?" I asked.

"You don't think it was just to become faceblind?"

"No."

She thought for a moment, staring out at the beach cottages on her side of the road. "I guess you could say I left for the same reason you stayed."

I assumed she was talking about Fran, but then she added, "I didn't want to be the person other people had made me into."

"And I did?"

She turned from the cottages to me. "Didn't you? Generous Trevor. Level-headed Trevor. Never-loses-his-temper Trevor."

"That's not true. You know that."

"It doesn't matter. People don't care how you see yourself. It's who people think you are that matters most to them. Turn against those expectations, and they turn against you."

WHEN OUR PARENTS first heard about what Keeley had done—she had sent an email to them, the same as me—they tried to talk her out of it. They flew from Prescott, where they'd moved a couple of years earlier for

faceless in gethsemane

Mom's emphysema, to Boulder, where Keeley was staying at a VFP post-op center.

Less than a day after their arrival—it could have been hours—my mother called in a panic. "You have to do something."

"Like what?"

"Talk to her. She listens to you."

"It's her choice," I said. Besides, I was pretty sure nothing I said at this point was going to change it.

"What are you saying?" my mother asked. "Are you saying you won't help? That you don't care?"

"Of course not."

"I've tried to reason with her." Earrings rattled as my mother shook her head. "But these people she's with, they've got her brainwashed. She refuses to listen to reason. Your father is about to have a heart attack."

"I told you going down there was a bad idea."

"It's all right. He's sedated. But I have to tell you, my blood pressure is acting up. I feel lightheaded."

"What do you want me to do?"

"Talk some sense into her." My mother's breath shuddered, loose as an unhinged door. "I just wish I knew what we did wrong."

"You didn't do anything wrong."

But she was inconsolable. "I don't know what we could have done any differently. I really don't."

"Take it easy, all right? Calm down. I'll see what I can do."

seeds of change

But of course it was too late. There was no way to reverse the procedure. It was like having a stroke, a bullet, or a piece of shrapnel, rip through that part of the brain. Once the microvilli were implanted, that was it. There was no going back.

I'd researched the procedure as soon as I heard from her, trying to find out as much as I could about what Keeley had done to herself.

The microvilli—nanoscopic synapses and neurons—rewired the fusiform face area of the visual cortex. This area was essentially a computational machine, wired into the visual cortex, that had several subcomponents. There were subcomponents for gender, skin color, features, and emotional expression. It turned out that you could short-circuit the neuroprocessor for skin color, while leaving the synapses for happiness or gender intact. In the same way, you could short-circuit the pattern recognition synapses for the nose, mouth, and eyes. The nanosurgery was very precise. Any of these features could be selected for. Most VFPs chose to have a standard set of facial elements grayed out—"blinded." But in theory any of the subcomponents of the cortex could be reconfigured.

"I don't know what we did to deserve this," my mother said when I called to tell her the news.

"You didn't do anything," I said.

"We should never have moved." It had been a major decision to relocate to Arizona. She hadn't wanted to go, but my father had insisted.

faceless in gethsemane

"She would have done it even if you'd stayed," I said. But it was no use, my mother was determined to blame herself, and by extension, my father.

"You don't know that," she said. "If we were still there, we might have been able to stop her."

"There are worse things she could have done," I said.

"Like what?"

"You know." Out of habit, I offered up a shrug. "Drugs. Prostitution. At least this is socially responsible."

"It's selfish, if you ask me."

I didn't ask her to explain. I didn't want to encourage her. I wanted her to accept what had happened and move on. It wasn't any of her business what Keeley or anyone else did. It was Keeley's life, not hers. But, like a lot of people, she didn't see it that way. She saw what Keeley did as a reflection of herself, something for which she would ultimately be judged.

"REMEMBER THAT TIME on the playground?" Keeley had said after our parents flew back to Prescott. She'd called to thank me for supporting her by not flying out and attempting to deprogram her. That was the word she used.

"Back in grade school?"

"Yeah. Behind the eucalyptus trees."

"Not very well," I said. Hoping she'd let it go at that.

"What did you see?"

I'd never told her. I'd never told anyone. "Nothing," I said.

seeds of change

"I don't believe you," she said. "We all see things. Whether we want to admit it or not. Things that embarrass us or scare us. Uncomfortable things. Things we'd rather forget."

"What difference does it make what I saw?"

"Because seeing isn't just believing," she said.

I waited for the other shoe to drop. But it didn't. She seemed lost in thought, and after a minute or two she let it go and we hung up.

FRAN WAS ON her best behavior. I had to give her that. She smiled when Keeley first walked up to the front door and into our house. Made polite inquires about the flight. Asked if Keeley wanted anything to eat or drink. Even so, she couldn't keep a lid on it. Not completely. Questions bubbled up.

"I don't see what you hope to accomplish," Fran said. "Who are you doing this for? That's what I want to know."

"Fran," I said. "Please." I had a bad feeling. I didn't know where this was headed. We sat in the living room, me and Fran on the antique sofa she had inherited from her mother, Keeley on a restored wingback chair, watching the coffee Fran had poured send up tendrils of steam.

"No," Keeley said. "It's all right." Her tone suggested that she'd prepared for this, willed it even. Being here was a test. If she could convince Fran, then she could convince anyone. That was why she'd come, the real reason she asked to stay with us. It didn't have anything to do with me.

faceless in gethsemane

"I'm doing this for myself," Keeley said. She stirred cream and sugar into the cup on the table in front of her.

"Even when the people effected by it don't want you to do it?" Fran asked. "Even if it's not how they want to be seen?"

"Some of them do."

"But not all. What about the people who don't? Shouldn't their wishes be taken into account?"

"I'm not stopping them from doing what they want," Keeley said. "I'm not preventing anyone from being, or expressing, who they are."

Fran cradled her coffee in her lap. She held it with both hands, wrapping her hands around the warmth. "By not seeing people the way they actually are, aren't you denying them their true identity?"

"Identity is more than physical appearance," Keeley said. "It's language and a lot of other factors. The surgery doesn't get rid of that."

"Then what's the point? I mean, what do any of the people you look at gain by you being faceblind?"

"Well for one thing I don't prejudge people the way I used to. I don't automatically assign a whole bunch of cultural baggage to someone based on a bunch of misconceptions, preconceptions, or stereotypes."

"Not everyone has that problem," Fran said.

"I'm not saying they do. All I'm saying is that I did, and I took steps to correct it. I didn't want to see the world the way I used to. Before the surgery, I'd look at a person

seeds of change

sometimes and misread them, see things that weren't there. Now, there aren't any facial miscues. I see people for who they really are."

"What about people who pretend to be something they aren't?" Fran asked.

"People lie about who they are all the time," Keeley said. "That's not my responsibility."

"It's not." Fran agreed. She paused. "I'm sorry you feel that way. I'm sorry you feel like you have to put the past behind you." She glanced over at me. "For some of us, the past is a source of strength, a way of knowing who we are."

"I'm not threatened by the past."

"Maybe not. But you haven't escaped it, either. Not really. You might see people differently, but people still see you the way they always did. That hasn't changed."

"If it makes you feel any better," Keeley said, "I've paid a price. I'll never see the faces of my children. I'll never be able to look into their eyes or see them smile."

Fran bit her lower lip. "I'm sorry for that, too."

And so on. It was hard to keep up with both sides of the discussion. One moment I leaned one way, the next the other. After a while, my head hurt.

"All this food for thought is making me hungry," I said. We'd been sitting there for almost two hours. It was getting close to six. "Is anyone else ready for dinner?"

"I could eat," Keeley said.

Fran, biting her lower lip, rose to clear the empty coffee cups from the table, taking them into the kitchen.

faceless in gethsemane

"We could go out for Chinese," I said, standing up to give her a hand.

Keeley trailed after us. "I'd like to stop by the library first," she said. "If that's all right. I want to drop off a couple new drawings I brought with me."

"I've never seen any of your stuff," I confessed. I'd been curious, sure. I could have looked it up online. But I hadn't. Why? Fran. I didn't want to rock the boat—ruin what we had.

"It's not all that different from the stuff I did back in school," Keeley said. She'd contributed to the quarterly webzine put out by the English department. Charcoal sketches. Drawings. A water color or two. She'd done people, mostly. Faces, up close and personal, that expressed an unsettling but vaguely familiar feeling, like the distorted but recognizable reflection in a funhouse mirror. That had always been her interest. The inner lives of people.

"You know what I mean," I said. "The stuff you've done since the surgery."

Keeley shrugged. "I didn't think you were interested."

Fran, wiping her hands on a dish towel, said, "I'll meet you out at the car. I want to get a jacket."

THE GROUP OF protestors in front of the library looked smaller. I didn't see the two wearing the hockey masks.

"You think they'd get tired or hungry," I said. What the group had lost in number, they made up for in enthusiasm.

seeds of change

Keeley nodded. She had been edgy on the drive over. Every time I glanced in the rearview mirror, I saw her peering out the window, the portfolio with her paintings clutched tightly, almost protectively, in her lap. As I parked in a space close to the main library entrance, an anxious face peered out at us from behind the tinted glass doors.

"Collin," Keeley said. "He's in charge of setup."

The man was small and nattily dressed, sporting a triangular goatee on a round, wire-rimmed head devoid of hair. He moved like a tap dancer, skipping in and out of view when Keeley opened her car door to get out.

"This won't take long," she said. "I'll be right back."

I opened my door. "I'm coming with you." I cut a glance at Fran.

"I think I'll wait here," Fran said. She was hunkered down in the passenger seat, the collar of her jacket pulled up around her neck and ears.

"Are you sure?" I said.

"Yes."

"Sure you don't want to at least check it out?" I said. "See for yourself what so many people are all up in arms about?"

"I can read about it."

"It's not the same as seeing it in person."

"I'm going to go on ahead," Keeley said, growing impatient.

"Fine," I said to Fran. No way I was going to let Keeley walk past the group on her own.

faceless in gethsemane

I slammed the door, locked the car, and hurried after Keeley. Behind me, I could feel Fran stewing, embarrassed and angry at me for having dragged her into this mess.

I kept my gaze lowered as we approached the protestors. "Don't look at them," I said under my breath. Looking at them, I imagined, would only provoke them. Like meeting a growling dog in the eye, it would be regarded as a challenge, an invitation for violence.

But Keeley did look. Not only that, she smiled and even waved. As an ambassador, it was her job.

There were catcalls, sure—"Erasist!" and "Face the Facts!"—but no spit, garbage, or rotten fruit. It could have been worse.

Then we were inside, whisked into the quiet sanctuary of the library by Collin and a security guard who quickly latched the door after us.

"THAT WASN'T TOO bad," Keeley said, looking back at the crowd.

"It will get worse," Collin said. "Believe me. This is just a precursor. Tomorrow, we'll have extra security and the police will be here."

The artwork had been set up at the back of the library on moveable partitions arranged in a zigzag pattern to create small alcoves. Sculpture, mounted on pedestals or placed directly on the floor, filled the space between the partitions. The work ranged from the photorealistic to the abstract. There were exquisitely detailed line drawings and anthropomorphic blobs. None of the heads had faces. Blank voids or empty hollows, eerily devoid of content but not expression, took the place of eyes, noses, and mouths.

I was nervous as we approached Keeley's. My palms were wet. I discreetly wiped them on my pants.

Keeley's latest work echoed the lovingly rendered portraits I remembered, but instead of eyes the faces offered different windows into the soul. Abstract squiggles. Dreamlike surrealisms. Impressionistic smudges. One painting in particular grabbed my attention. "Gesthemane." In it, a young woman pirouetted in a walled garden, scarecrow-like, her arms held out as if nailed to an invisible cross. The garden was barren—little more than a vacant lot—and her face reflected the crumbling stone enclosure, desolate except for a tiny green sprout emerging from a crack.

As I gazed at the picture, Keeley unwrapped the two she had brought with her.

"Well?" Keeley said as Collin prepared to hang them with other pieces.

"I don't know," I admitted. I wasn't sure what I thought—or what I'd expected from the artwork.

"Tell me," Keeley said. "The first thing that came to your mind. Don't think about it."

"I don't know if it's going to change peoples' minds," I said. "I don't know if any of this is going to make most people feel better about who you are and what you're trying to accomplish."

faceless in gethsemane

"It's not supposed to," Collin said.

I shook my head, confused. "Then what's the point?"

"To challenge people," Keeley said.

"Challenge them how?"

"To see the world differently." Keeley waved a hand at the surrounding art. "To see themselves differently."

"People don't want to see themselves," I said. I thought of Fran. "They don't want to be challenged. They want to be reassured. They don't want to feel threatened. They want to be told everything will be all right, even if it's not."

"What about you?" Keeley said. "Is that what you want?"

"I don't know." But I did know. I looked around at the faceless portraits. I couldn't tell who any of these people were, or who they had been. They had been stripped of their pasts. It was hard to see the future they inhabited. "It seems lonely," I said. "If you don't know who you were, how do you know who you should be?"

"You can be anyone you want," Keeley said. "That's the point. After the surgery, you're not tied to the past."

"You're free," Collin said. His face ballooned close to mine, buoyed by the same fervent intensity. I don't know what he saw when he looked at me. Maybe he saw what he wanted. Or maybe he saw what was in Keeley's latest pictures.

They were of me. Not literally, but figuratively. I recognized myself in the entoptic collages that gave expression to the faces. The actinic flashes of light, and slow lava

seeds of change

lamp turmoil of one world bleeding across the retina to reveal, and possibly become, another.

Looking at those pictures, free was the last thing I felt.

WHAT I SAW that day behind the eucalyptus trees—with my eyes squeezed tight and my fingers pressing against my lids—was Steve.

Dead.

His head split open under my fingertips, exploding into a mist of roiling green and purple.

I wanted to let go but I couldn't. I was paralyzed, struck by the shocking clarity of the face that had emerged from the seething pattern of light. It was like a ghost, invisible to the naked eye, suddenly showing up in a photograph.

Two days later the vision came true. Steve died in a playground accident. He was running to catch a fly ball and collided with another kid. They smacked heads. Steve was knocked unconscious. An ambulance came and took him to the hospital, but he never woke up, even when Myrtle Baumgarten visited and kissed him on the cheek. After two days in a coma, he succumbed, killed by a bone splinter that had worked its way into his brain.

It was a coincidence, of course. I knew that. I hadn't seen the future, or caused it. The whole thing had the quality of a dream, like the time I plummeted from the top of the huge tree behind our house. I didn't know if I'd actually slipped—if I'd managed to grab onto the last limb before hitting the ground and killing myself—or if I only

faceless in gethsemane

imagined I did. That was what I saw when I looked at Keeley's faces. What would other people see? Sometimes, the things we see are in ourselves. They come from inside us, not the world outside.

"ARE YOU ALL right?" Keeley asked on the way out of the library.

"Sure. Why wouldn't I be?"

"You look pale."

I shrugged. "Just sugar crashing," I said. "Get a little food in me, and I'll be fine."

"You sure?"

I sagged to a halt in front of the door while I waited for the security guard to let us out. Collin had stayed behind to put the finishing touches on the exhibit. "It's been hard," I said.

"What?"

I glanced at the protestors, then back to the stacks of books in the direction of the exhibit. "All of this."

"Dealing with me, you mean. And Fran."

"It hasn't been easy."

"Well, I appreciate it," she said. "Really. I'm not just saying that. I don't know what I would have done without you."

"What do you mean?"

"You've done a lot for me over the years, meant a lot to me. I mean that. Without you, I wouldn't be the person I am. I wouldn't have done the things I have."

seeds of change

What was she saying? Was she saying that I was responsible for what she'd done to herself?

"I wish we had more time to talk," she went on. "Just the two of us, I mean. You know. Without any distractions. Without all of this." She let out a breath as the security guard pulled open the door, exposing us to the chants of the protesters. "Just you and me. Brother and sister. The way we used, back when we were kids and there were no secrets between us."

I nodded, even though I knew it wouldn't happen anytime soon. Still, it was nice to think it was possible—that Keeley believed it was possible.

AS SOON AS Keely and I got back in the car, Fran said, "I want to go home." Just like that. Her mind was made up. She stared straight ahead, her jaw set, looking at nothing as far as I could tell.

"What's the matter?" I asked. "What happened?" Behind me, Keeley's seatbelt clicked.

"Nothing happened," Fran said. "Why do you always want to know if something happened?"

"You lost your appetite," I said. "There must be a reason."

"I wasn't really hungry," Fran said. "I wasn't ready to eat dinner. You're the one who wanted to go out, not me. I just came along for the ride."

"You didn't have to," I said. "No one made you. You could have stayed home if that's what you wanted."

faceless in gethsemane

"I've done as much as I can," she said. She pressed the heels of her hands to her forehead. "I tried. I really did. I can't do any more."

"So what are you saying?"

"I just want to go home. That's all."

"Now?"

"Yes. We've got leftover lasagna in the freezer. I can heat that up. Make a salad, or whatever."

"I like lasagna," Keeley said. "Lasagna's fine with me. And I'm more tired than I thought. A quiet evening might not be a bad idea."

WE HEARD THE sirens when we were still a few blocks away. By the time we got to the house, it was in flames.

I parked a couple of houses down from the fire trucks. I felt numb and sick to my stomach. As soon as the car stopped, Fran jumped out.

"Wait!" I said. "What are you doing?"

She ignored me or didn't hear me. I hopped out and ran after her, catching her by the arm as she passed the first fire truck, dragging her to a stop.

"There's nothing you can do," I gasped. It was obviously too late. The fire was spreading fast. I could feel the flames on my face, the skin tightening under the heat. I thought I could smell gasoline in the air. Flames billowed out of the windows and thick gouts of smoke darkened the sky. Then there was an explosion somewhere inside of the flames and one whole side of the house disinte-

seeds of change

grated in a shower of embers.

"My God," Fran said. She turned to Keeley, who'd joined us. "Look what you've done."

"I didn't do anything."

"Yes, you did." Fran jabbed a finger at her. "You came back. If you hadn't come back, none of this would have happened."

"That's not true," Keeley said.

"You could have minded your own damn business," Fran said. "Instead, you had to drag us into it." She bunched her hands into fists. "What if we'd been in there? We'd be dead by now." Tears flickered down her cheeks.

I went to her. She stiffened as I put an arm around her and pulled her close. "It's all right," I said. "Everything will be fine."

"No, it won't." She sniffed and wiped at the tears with white knuckles. "Nothing will ever be the same again. We've lost everything."

"We're alive," I said. "No one got hurt."

"Our life here is ruined."

"We can start a new life," I said.

She rested her forehead on my shoulder. "I don't want to start a new life. I want the life we had."

Keeley stood a few feet off to one side, watching the house burn. I could see the flames in her eyes. It looked like the fire was burning in her. I turned back to the house. The flames were bright, as if the whole world was on fire.

People went away. When they came back, you never

knew what to expect. Not from them, and sometimes not from yourself.

I closed my eyes against the glare. I kept my eyes shut for a few beats. My heart thudded in my chest and my mouth was dry. I pressed my fingertips to my eyelids and started to count to ten.

spider the artist

>>>

Nnedi Okorafor-Mbachu is the author of the novels Zahrah the Windseeker *and* The Shadow Speaker. *Her forthcoming book for children,* Long Juju Man, *recently won the Macmillan Writer's Prize for Africa. She has also been an NAACP Image Award and Andre Norton Award nominee, as well as a finalist for the* Essence Magazine *Literary Award. Her short fiction has appeared in* Strange Horizons *and in anthologies such as* So Long Been Dreaming *and* Dark Matter: Reading the Bones.

Like much of Okorafor-Mbachu's fiction, this story takes place in Africa. "Nigeria is one of the top oil-producing countries in the world. Yet this fact has been more a curse than a blessing," Okorafor-Mbachu said. "The Niger Delta has one of the highest concentrations of biodiversity on Earth, yet it is an environmental, political, and social mess. Oil spills, gas flares, pipeline explosions, poor land management, human rights abuses, the oil companies and the Nigerian government could care less about the land or people."

spider the artist

nnedi okorafor-mbachu

Zombie no go go, unless you tell am to go
Zombie!
Zombie!
Zombie no go stop, unless you tell am to stop
Zombie no go turn, unless you tell am to turn
Zombie!
Zombie no go think, unless you tell am to think
   —from *Zombie* by Fela Kuti, Nigerian musician
      and self-proclaimed voice of the voiceless

spider the artist

y husband used to beat me. That was how I ended up out there that evening behind our house, just past the bushes, through the tall grass, in front of the pipelines. Our small house was the last in the village, practically in the forest itself. So nobody ever saw or heard him beating me.

Going out there was the best way to put space between me and him without sending him into further rage. When I went behind the house, he knew where I was and he knew I was alone. But he was too full of himself to realize I was thinking about killing myself.

My husband was a drunk, like too many of the members of the Niger Delta People's Movement. It was how they all controlled their anger and feelings of helplessness. The fish, shrimps and crayfish in the creeks were dying. Drinking the water shriveled women's wombs and eventually made men urinate blood.

There was a stream where I had been fetching water. A flow station was built nearby and now the stream was rank and filthy, with an oily film that reflected rainbows. Cassava and yam farms yielded less and less each year. The air left your skin dirty and smelled like something preparing to die. In some places, it was always daytime because of the noisy gas flares.

seeds of change

My village was shit.

On top of all this, People's Movement members were getting picked off like flies. The "kill-and-go" had grown bold. They shot People's Movement members in the streets, they ran them over, dragged them into the swamps. You never saw them again.

I tried to give my husband some happiness. But after three years, my body continued to refuse him children. It's easy to see the root of his frustration and sadness . . . but pain is pain. And he dealt it to me regularly.

My greatest, my only true possession was my father's guitar. It was made of fine polished Abura timber and it had a lovely tortoiseshell pick guard. Excellent handwork. My father said that the timber used to create the guitar came from one of the last timber trees in the delta. If you held it to your nose, you could believe this. The guitar was decades old and still smelled like fresh cut wood, like it wanted to tell you its story because only it could.

I wouldn't exist without my father's guitar. When he was a young man, he used to sit in front of the compound in the evening and play for everyone. People danced, clapped, shut their eyes and listened. Cell phones would ring and people would ignore them. One day, it was my mother who stopped to listen.

I used to stare at my father's fast long-fingered hands when he played. Oh, the harmonies. He could weave anything with his music—rainbows, sunrises, spider webs sparkling with morning dew. My older brothers weren't

spider the artist

interested in learning how to play. But I was, so my father taught me everything he knew. And now it was my long-fingers that graced the strings. I'd always been able to hear music and my fingers moved even faster than my father's. I was good. Really good.

But I married that stupid man. Andrew. So I only played behind the house. Away from him. My guitar was my escape.

That fateful evening, I was sitting on the ground in front of the fuel pipeline. It ran right through everyone's backyard. My village was an oil village, as was the village where I grew up. My mother lived in a similar village before she was married, as did her mother. We are Pipeline People.

My mother's grandmother was known for lying on the pipeline running through her village. She'd stay like that for hours, listening and wondering what magical fluids were running through the large never-ending steel tubes. This was before the Zombies, of course. I laughed. If she tried to lie on a pipeline now she'd be brutally killed.

Anyway, when I was feeling especially blue, I'd take my guitar and come out here and sit right in front of the pipeline. I knew I was flirting with death by being so close but when I was like this, I didn't really care. I actually welcomed the possibility of being done with life. It was a wonder that my husband didn't smash my guitar during one of his drunken rages. I'd surely have quickly thrown myself on the pipeline if he did. Maybe that was why he'd rather smash my nose than my guitar.

seeds of change

This day, he'd only slapped me hard across the face. I had no idea why. He'd simply come in, seen me in the kitchen and smack! Maybe he'd had a bad day at work— he worked very hard at a local restaurant. Maybe one of his women had scorned him. Maybe I did something wrong. I didn't know. I didn't care. My nose was just starting to stop bleeding and I was not seeing so many stars.

My feet were only inches from the pipeline. I was especially daring this night. It was warmer and more humid than normal. Or maybe it was my stinging burning face. The mosquitoes didn't even bother me much. In the distance, I could see Nneka, a woman who rarely spoke to me, giving her small sons a bath in a large tub. Some men were playing cards at a table several houses down. It was dark, there were small small trees and bushes here and even our closest neighbor was not very close, so I was hidden.

I sighed and placed my hands on the guitar strings. I plucked out a tune my father used to play. I sighed and closed my eyes. I would always miss my father. The feel of the strings vibrating under my fingers was exquisite.

I fell deep into the zone of my music, weaving it, then floating on a glorious sunset that lit the palm tree tops and . . .

Click!

I froze. My hands still on the strings, the vibration dying. I didn't dare move. I kept my eyes closed. The side of my face throbbed.

spider the artist

Click! This time the sound was closer. *Click!* Closer. *Click!* Closer.

My heart pounded and I felt nauseous with fear. Despite my risk taking, I knew this was not the way I wanted to die. Who would want to be torn limb from limb by Zombies? As everyone in my village did multiple times a day, I quietly cursed the Nigerian government.

Twing!

The vibration of the guitar string was stifled by my middle finger still pressing it down. My hands started to shake, but still I kept my eyes shut. Something sharp and cool lifted my finger. I wanted to scream. The string was plucked again.

Twang!

The sound was deeper and fuller, my finger no longer muffling the vibration. Very slowly, I opened my eyes. My heart skipped. The thing stood about three feet tall, which meant I was eye-to-eye with it. I'd never seen one up close. Few people have. These things are always running up and down the pipeline like a herd of super fast steer, always with things to do.

I chanced a better look. It really *did* have eight legs. Even in the darkness, those legs shined, catching even the dimmest light. A bit more light and I'd have been able to see my face perfectly reflected back at me. I'd heard that they polished and maintained themselves. This made even more sense now, for who would have time to keep them looking so immaculate?

seeds of change

The government came up with the idea to create the Zombies, and Shell, Chevron and a few other oil companies (who were just as desperate) supplied the money to pay for it all. The Zombies were made to combat pipeline bunkering and terrorism. It makes me laugh. The government and the oil people destroyed our land and dug up our oil, then they created robots to keep us from taking it back.

They were originally called Anansi Droids 419 but we call them "oyibo contraption" and, most often, Zombie, the same name we call those "kill-and-go" soldiers who come in here harassing us every time something bites their brains.

It's said that Zombies can think. Artificial Intelligence, this is called. I have had some schooling, a year or two of university, but my area was not in the sciences. No matter my education, as soon as I got married and brought to this damn place I became like every other woman here, a simple village woman living in the delta region where Zombies kill anyone who touches the pipelines and whose husband knocks her around every so often. What did I know about Zombie intellect?

It looked like a giant shiny metal spider. It moved like one too. All smooth-shifting joints and legs. It crept closer and leaned in to inspect my guitar strings some more. As it did so, two of its back legs tapped on the metal of the pipeline. *Click! Click! Click!*

It pushed my thumb back down on the strings and plucked the string twice, making a muted *pluck!* It looked

spider the artist

at me with its many blue shining round eyes. Up close I could see that they weren't lights. They were balls of a glowing metallic blue undulating liquid, like charged mercury. I stared into them fascinated. No one else in my village could possibly know this fact. No one had gotten close enough. *Eyes of glowing bright blue liquid metal*, I thought. *Na wa*.

It pressed my hand harder and I gasped, blinking and looking away from its hypnotic eyes. Then I understood.

"You . . . you want me to play?"

It sat there waiting, placing a leg on the body of my guitar with a soft tap. It had been a long time since anyone had wanted me to play for him. I played my favorite highlife song. "Love Dey See Road" by Oliver De Coque. I played like my life depended on it.

The Zombie didn't move, its leg remaining pressed to my guitar. Was it listening? I was sure it was. Twenty minutes later, when I stopped finally playing, sweat running down my face, it touched the tips of my aching hands. Gently.

SOME OF THESE pipelines carry diesel fuel, others carry crude oil. Millions of liters of it a day. Nigeria supplies twenty-five percent of United States oil. And we get virtually nothing in return. Nothing but death by Zombie attack. We can all tell you stories.

When the Zombies were first released, no one knew about them. All people would hear were rumors about peo-

seeds of change

ple getting torn apart near pipelines or sightings of giant white spiders in the night. Or you'd hear about huge pipeline explosions, charred bodies everywhere. But the pipeline where the bodies lay would be perfectly intact.

People still bunkered. My husband was one of them. I suspected that he sold the fuel and oil on the black market; he would bring some of the oil home, too. You let it sit in a bucket for two days and it would become something like kerosene. I used it for cooking. So I couldn't really complain. But bunkering was a very very dangerous practice.

There were ways of breaking a pipeline open without immediately bringing the wrath of Zombies. My husband and his comrades used some sort of powerful laser cutter. They stole them from the hospitals. But they had to be very very quiet when cutting through the metal. All it took was one bang, one vibration, and the Zombies would come running within a minute. Many of my husband's comrades had been killed because of the tap of someone's wedding ring or the tip of the laser cutter on steel.

Two years ago a group of boys had been playing too close to the pipeline. Two of them were wrestling and they fell on it. Within seconds the Zombies came. One boy managed to scramble away. But the other was grabbed by the arm and flung into some bushes. His arm and both of his legs were broken. Government officials *said* that Zombies were programmed to do as little harm as possible but . . . I didn't believe this, *na lie*.

spider the artist

They were terrible creatures. To get close to a pipeline was to risk a terrible death. Yet the goddamn things ran right through our backyards.

But I didn't care. My husband was beating the hell out of me during these months. I don't know why. He had not lost his job. I knew he was seeing other women. We were poor but we were not starving. Maybe it was because I couldn't bear him children. It is my fault I know, but what can I do?

I found myself out in the backyard more and more. And this particular Zombie visited me every time. I loved playing for it. It would listen. Its lovely eyes would glow with joy. Could a robot feel joy? I believed intelligent ones like this could. Many times a day, I would see a crowd of Zombies running up and down the pipeline, off to do repairs or policing, whatever they did. If my Zombie was amongst them, I couldn't tell.

It was about the tenth time it visited me that it did something very very strange. My husband had come home smelling practically flammable, stinking of several kinds of alcohol—beer, palm wine, perfume. I had been thinking hard all day. About my life. I was stuck. I wanted a baby. I wanted to get out of the house. I wanted a job. I wanted friends. I needed courage. I knew I had courage. I had faced a Zombie, many times.

I was going to ask my husband about teaching at the elementary school. I'd heard that they were looking for teachers. When he walked in, he greeted me with a sloppy

seeds of change

hug and kiss and then plopped himself on the couch. He turned on the television. It was late but I brought him his dinner, pepper soup heavy with goat meat, chicken and large shrimp. He was in a good drunken mood. But as I stood there watching him eat, all my courage fled. All my need for change skittered and cowered to the back of my brain.

"Do you want anything else?" I asked.

He looked up at me and actually smiled. "The soup is good today."

I smiled, but something inside me ducked its head lower. "I'm glad," I said. I picked up my guitar. "I'm going to the back. It's nice outside."

"Don't go too close to the pipeline," he said. But he was looking at the TV and gnawing on a large piece of goat meat.

I crept into the darkness, through the bushes and grasses, to the pipeline. I sat in my usual spot. A foot from it. I strummed softly, a series of chords. A forlorn tune that spoke my heart. Where else was there to go from here? Was this my life? I sighed. I hadn't been to church in a month.

When it came clicking down the pipe, my heart lifted. Its blue liquid eyes glowed strong tonight. There was a woman from whom I once bought a bolt of blue cloth. The cloth was a rich blue that reminded me of the open water on sunny days. The woman said the cloth was "azure." My Zombie's eyes were a deep azure this night.

spider the artist

It stopped, standing before me. Waiting. I knew it was my Zombie because a month ago, it had allowed me to put a blue butterfly sticker on one of its front legs.

"Good evening," I said.

It did not move.

"I'm sad today," I said.

It stepped off the pipeline, its metal legs clicking on the metal and then whispering on the dirt and grass. It sat its body on the ground as it always did. Then it waited.

I strummed a few chords and then played its favorite song, Bob Marley's "No Woman No Cry." As I played, its body slowly began to rotate, something I'd come to understand was its way of expressing pleasure. I smiled. When I stopped playing, it turned its eyes back to me. I sighed, strummed an A minor chord, and sat back. "My life is shit," I said.

Suddenly, it rose up on its eight legs with a soft whir. It stretched and straightened its legs until it was standing a foot taller than normal. From under its body in the center, something whitish and metallic began to descend. I gasped, grabbing my guitar. My mind told me to move away. Move away fast. I'd befriended this artificial creature. I knew it. Or I thought I knew it. But what did I really know about why it did what it did? Or why it came to me?

The metallic substance descended faster, pooling in the grass beneath it. I squinted. The stuff was wire. Right before my eyes, I watched the Zombie take this wire and do something with five of its legs while it supported itself on

seeds of change

the other three. The legs scrambled around, working and weaving the shiny wire this way and that. They moved too fast for me to see exactly what they were creating. Grass flew and the soft whirring sound grew slightly louder.

Then the legs stopped. For a moment all I could hear was the sounds of crickets and frogs singing, the breeze blowing in the palm and mangrove tree tops. I could smell the sizzling oil of someone frying plantain or yam nearby.

My eyes focused on what the Zombie had done. I grinned. I grinned and grinned. "What is that?" I whispered.

It held it up with two of its front legs and tapped its back leg twice on the ground as it always seemed to when it was trying to make a point. A point that I usually didn't understand.

It brought three legs forward and commenced to pluck out what first was a medley of my favorite songs, from Bob Marley to Sunny Ade to Carlos Santana. Then its music deepened to something so complex and beautiful that I was reduced to tears of joy, awe, ecstasy. People must have heard the music, maybe they looked out their windows or opened their doors. But we were hidden by the darkness, the grass, the trees. I cried and cried. I don't know why, but I cried. I wonder if it was pleased by my reaction. I think it was.

I spent the next hour learning to play its tune.

TEN DAYS LATER, a group of Zombies attacked some oil workers and soldiers deep in the delta. Ten of the men

spider the artist

were torn limb from limb, their bloody remains scattered all over the swampy land. Those who escaped told reporters that nothing would stop the Zombies. A soldier had even thrown a grenade at one, but the thing protected itself with the very force field it had been built to use during pipeline explosions. The soldier said the force field looked like a crackling bubble made of lightning.

"*Wahala!* Trouble!" the soldier frantically told television reporters. His face was greasy with sweat and the sides of his eyes were twitching. "Evil, evil things! I've believed this from start! Look at me with grenade! *Ye ye!* I could do nothing!"

The pipeline the men had barely even started was found fully assembled. Zombies are made to make repairs, not fully assemble things. It was bizarre. Newspaper write-ups said that the Zombies were getting too smart for their own good. That they were rebelling. Something had certainly changed.

"Maybe it's only a matter of time before the damn things kill us all," my husband said, a beer in hand, as he read about the incident in the newspaper.

I considered never going near my Zombie again. They were unpredictable and possibly out of control.

IT WAS MIDNIGHT and I was out there again.

My husband hadn't laid a heavy hand on me in weeks. I think he sensed the change in me. I had changed. He now heard me play more. Even in the house. In the mornings.

seeds of change

After cooking his dinners. In the bedroom when his friends were over. And he was hearing songs that I knew gave him a most glorious feeling. As if each chord, each sound were examined by scientists and handpicked to provoke the strongest feeling of happiness.

My Zombie had solved my marital problems. At least the worst of them. My husband could not beat me when there was beautiful music sending his senses to lush, sweet places. I began to hope. To hope for a baby. Hope that I would one day leave my house and wifely duties for a job as music teacher at the elementary school. Hope that my village would one day reap from the oil being reaped from it. And I dreamt about being embraced by deep blue liquid metal, webs of wire and music.

I'd woken up that night from one of these strange dreams. I opened my eyes, a smile on my face. Good things were certainly coming. My husband was sleeping soundly beside me. In the dim moonlight, he looked so peaceful. His skin no longer smelled of alcohol. I leaned forward and kissed his lips. He didn't wake. I slipped out of bed and put on some pants and a long sleeve shirt. The mosquitoes would be out tonight. I grabbed my guitar.

I'd named my Zombie Udide Okwanka. In my language, it means "spider the artist." According to legend, Udide Okwanka is the Supreme Artist. And she lives underground where she takes fragments of things and changes them into something else. She can even weave spirits from straw. It was a good name for my Zombie. I wondered what Udide named me. I was sure it named me something, though I doubted that it told the others about me. I don't think it would have been allowed to keep seeing me.

Udide was waiting for me there, as if it sensed I would come out this night. I grinned, my heart feeling so warm. I sat down as it left the pipeline and crept up to me. It carried its instrument on top of its head. A sort of complex star made of wire. Over the weeks, it had added more wire lines, some thin and some thick. I often wondered where it put this thing when it was running about with the others, for the instrument was too big to hide on its body.

Udide held it before its eyes. With a front leg, it plucked out a sweet simple tune that almost made me weep with joy. It conjured up images of my mother and father, when they were so young and full of hope, when my brothers and I were too young to marry and move away. Before the "kill and go" had driven my oldest brother away to America and my middle brother to the north . . . when there was so much potential.

I laughed and wiped away a tear and started strumming some chords to support the tune. From there we took off into something so intricate, enveloping, intertwining . . . *Chei!* I felt as if I was communing with God. Ah-ah, this machine and me. You can't imagine.

"Eme!"

Our music instantly fell apart.

"Eme!" my husband called again.

seeds of change

I froze, staring at Udide who was also motionless. "Please," I whispered to it. "Don't hurt him."

"Samuel messaged me!" my husband said, his eyes still on his cell phone, as he stepped up to me through the tall grass. "There's a break in the pipeline near the school! Not a goddamn Zombie in sight yet! Throw down that guitar, woman! Let's go and get . . . " He looked up. A terrified look took hold of his face.

For a very long time it seemed we all were frozen in time. My husband standing just at the last of the tall grass. Udide standing in front of the pipeline, instrument held up like a ceremonial shield. And me between the two of them, too afraid to move. I turned to my husband. "Andrew," I said with the greatest of care. "Let me explain . . . "

He slowly dragged his gaze to me and gave me a look, as if he was seeing me for the first time. "My own wife?!" he whispered.

"I . . . "

Udide raised its two front legs. For a moment it looked almost like it was pleading with me. Or maybe offering me a hug. Then it clicked its legs together so hard that it produced a large red spark and an ear splitting *ting!*

My husband and I clapped our hands over our ears. The air instantly smelled like freshly lit matches. Even through the palms of my hands, I could hear the responses from down the pipeline. The clicking was so numerous that it sounded like a rain of tiny pebbles falling on the pipeline. Udide shuddered, scrambled back and stood on it, waiting. They came in a great mob. About twenty of them. The first thing that I noticed was their eyes. They were all a deep angry red.

The others scrambled around Udide, tapping their feet in complex rhythms on the pipe. I couldn't see Udide's eyes. Then they all ran off with amazing speed, to the east.

I turned to my husband. He was gone.

WORD SPREAD LIKE a disease because almost everyone had a cell phone. Soon everyone was clicking away on them, messaging things like, "Pipeline burst, near school! No Zombies in sight!" and "Hurry to school, bring bucket!" My husband never let me have my own cell phone. We couldn't afford one and he didn't think I needed one. But I knew where the elementary school was.

People now believed that the Zombies had all gone rogue, shrugging off their man-given jobs to live in the delta swamps and do whatever it was they did there. Normally, if bunkerers broke open a pipeline, even for the quietest jobs, the Zombies would become aware of it within an hour and repair the thing within another hour. But two hours later this broken pipe continued to splash fuel. That was when someone had decided to put the word out.

I knew better. The Zombies weren't "zombies" at all. They were thinking creatures. Smart beasts. They had a method to their madness. And most of them did not like human beings.

seeds of change

The chaos was lit by the headlights of several cars and trucks. The pipeline here was raised as it traveled south. Someone had taken advantage of this and removed a whole section of piping. Pink diesel fuel poured out of both ends like a giant fountain. People crowded beneath the flow like parched elephants, filling jerri cans, bottles, bowls, buckets. One man even held a garbage bag, until the fuel ate through the bag, splashing fuel all over the man's chest and legs.

The spillage collected into a large dark pink pool that swiftly flowed toward the elementary school, gathering on the playground. The fumes hit me even before I got within sight of the school. My eyes watered and my nose started running. I held my shirt over my nose and mouth. This barely helped.

People came in cars, motorcycles, buses, on foot. Everyone was messaging on their cell phones, further spreading the word. It had been a while since people who did not make a career out of fuel theft had gotten a sip of free fuel.

There were children everywhere. They ran up and down, sent on errands by their parents or just hanging around to be a part of the excitement. They'd probably never seen people able to go near a pipeline without getting killed. Hip-hop and highlife blasted from cars and SUVs with enhanced sound systems. The baseline vibrations were almost as stifling as the fumes. I had not a doubt that the Zombies knew this was going on.

spider the artist

I spotted my husband. He was heading toward the fountain of fuel with a large red bucket. Five men started arguing amongst each other. Two of them started pushing and shoving, almost falling into the fountain.

"Andrew!" I called over all the noise.

He turned. When he saw me, he narrowed his eyes.

"Please!" I said. "I'm . . . I'm sorry."

He spat and started walking away.

"You have to get out of here!" I said. "They will come!"

He whirled around and strode up to me. "How the hell are you so sure? Did you bring them yourself?"

As if in response, people suddenly started screaming and running. I cursed. The Zombies were coming from the street, forcing people to run toward the pool of fuel. I cursed, again. My husband was glaring at me. He pointed into my face with a look of disgust. I couldn't hear what he said over all the noise. He turned and ran off.

I tried to spot Udide amongst the Zombies. All of their eyes were still red. Was Udide even amongst them? I stared at their legs, searching for the butterfly sticker. There it was. Closest to me, to the left. "Udide!" I called.

As the name came out of my mouth, I saw two of the Zombies in the center each raise two front legs. My smile went to an "O" of shock. I dropped to the ground and threw my hands over my head. People were still splashing across the pool of fuel, trying to get into the school. Their cars continued blasting hip-hop and highlife, the headlights

seeds of change

still on, lighting the madness.

The two Zombies clicked their legs together, producing two large sparks. *Ting!*

WHOOOOOOOOSH!

I REMEMBER LIGHT, heat, the smell of burning hair and flesh and screams that melted to guttural gurgles. The noise was muffled. The stench was awful. My head to my lap, I remained in this hellish limbo for a long long time.

I'LL NEVER TEACH music at the elementary school. It was incinerated along with many of the children who went to it. My husband was killed, too. He died thinking I was some sort of spy fraternizing with the enemy . . . or something like that. Everyone died. Except me. Just before the explosion happened, Udide ran to me. It protected me with its force field.

So I lived.

And so did the baby inside me. The baby that my body allowed to happen because of Udide's lovely soothing music. Udide tells me it is a girl. How can a robot know this? Udide and I play for her every day. I can only imagine how content she is. But what kind of world will I be bringing her into? Where only her mother and Udide stand between a flat-out war between the Zombies and the human beings who created them?

Pray that Udide and I can convince man and droid to call a truce, otherwise the delta will keep rolling in blood, metal and flames. You know what else? You should also pray that these Zombies don't build themselves some fins and travel across the ocean.

resistance
> > >

Tobias S. Buckell is the author of the novels Crystal Rain, Ragamuffin, *and* Sly Mongoose. *He is a Writers of the Future winner, and has published more than thirty short stories, which have appeared in magazines including* Nature, Science Fiction Age, *and* Analog, *and in anthologies such as* Mojo: Conjure Stories, New Voices in Science Fiction, *and* I, Alien. *A collection of his short fiction,* Tides from the New Worlds, *is scheduled to appear in 2008.*

This story, which explores the importance of voting and the overthrowing of dictators, hits close to home for Buckell: he was born in 1979, during a coup d'état in Grenada. "In 1979 the revolution started with high hopes and big plans," Buckell said. "But as time dragged on some consolidated power, and with their sweeping reforms, also fell into the spiral of quashing opposition to the point where it became draconian and people ended up lined up against walls and shot."

resistance

Tobias S. Buckell

Four days after the coup Stanuel was ordered to fake an airlock pass. The next day he waited inside a cramped equipment locker large enough to hold two people while an armed rover the size and shape of a helmet wafted around the room, twisting and counter-rotating pieces of itself as it scanned the room briefly. Stanuel held his breath and willed himself not to move or make a sound. He just floated in place, thankful for the lack of

resistance

gravity that might have betrayed him had he needed to depend on locked, nervous muscles.

The rover gave up and returned to the corridor, the airlock door closing behind it. Stanuel slipped back out. The rover had missed him because he'd been fully suited-up for vacuum. No heat signature.

Behind the rover's lenses had been the eyes of Pan. And since the coup, anyone knew better than to get noticed by Pan. Even the airlock pass cut it too close. He would disappear when Pan's distributed networks noticed what he'd done.

By then, Pan would not be a problem.

Stanuel checked his suit over again, then cycled the airlock out. The outer door split in two and pulled apart.

But where was the man Stanuel was supposed to bring in?

He realized there was an inky blackness in the space just outside the ring of the lock. A blotch that grew larger, and then tumbled in. The suit flickered, and turned a dull gray to match the general interior color of the airlock.

The person stood up, and Stanuel repressurized the airlock.

They waited as Stanuel snapped seals and took his own helmet off. He hung the suit up in the locker he'd just been hiding in. "We have to hurry, we only have about ten minutes before the next rover patrol."

Behind him, Stanuel heard crinkling and crunching. When he turned around the spacesuit had disappeared. He

seeds of change

now faced a tall man with dark skin and long dreadlocks past his shoulders, and eyes as gray as the bench behind him. The spacesuit had turned into a long, black trenchcoat. "Rovers?" the man asked.

Stanuel held his hand up and glyphed a 3-D picture in the air above his palm. The man looked at the rover spin and twist and shoot. "Originally they were station maintenance bots. Semi-autonomous remote operated vehicles. Now they're armed."

"I see." The man pulled a large backpack off his shoulders and unzipped it.

"So . . . what now?" Stanuel asked.

The gray eyes flicked up from the pack. "You don't know?"

"I'm part of a cell. But we run distributed tasks, only checking it with people who assign them. It keeps us insulated. I was only told to open this airlock and let you in. You would know what comes next. Is the attack tonight? Should I get armed? Are you helping the attack?"

The man opened the pack all the way to reveal a small arsenal of guns, grenades, explosives, and—oddly—knives. Very large knives. He looked up at Stanuel. "I *am* the attack. I've been asked to shut Pan down."

"But you're not a programmer . . ."

"I can do all things through explosives, who destroy for me." The man began moving the contents of the pack inside the pockets and straps of the trenchcoat, clipped more to his belt and thigh, as well as to holsters under

resistance

each arm, and then added pieces to his ankles.

He was now a walking arsenal.

But only half the pack had been emptied. The mysterious mercenary tossed it at Stanuel. "Besides, you're going to help."

Stanuel coughed. "Me?"

"According to the resistance message, you're a maintenance manager, recently promoted. You still know all the sewer lines, access ducts, and holes required to get me to the tower. How long do you guess we have before it notices your unauthorized use of an airlock?"

"An hour," Stanuel said. The last time he'd accidentally gone somewhere Pan didn't like, rovers had been in his office within an hour.

"And can we get to the tower within an hour, Stanuel, without being noticed?"

Stanuel nodded.

The large, well-armed man pointed at the airlock door into the corridor. "Well, let's not dally."

"Can I ask you something?" Stanuel asked.

"Yes."

"Your name. You know mine. I don't know yours."

"Pepper," said the mercenary. "Now can we leave?"

A SINGLE TINY sound ended the secrecy of their venture: the buzz of wings. Pepper's head snapped in the direction of the sound, locks spinning out from his head.

seeds of change

He slapped his palm against the side of the wall, crushing a butterfly-like machine perfectly flat.

"A bug," Stanuel said.

Pepper launched down the corridor, bouncing off the walls until he hit the bulkhead at the far end. He glanced around the corner. "Clear."

"Pan knows you're in Haven now." Stanuel felt fear bloom, an instant explosion of paralysis that left him hanging in the air. "It will mobilize."

"Then get me into the tower, quick. Let's go, Stanuel, we're not engaged in something that rewards the slow."

But Stanuel remained in place. "They chose me because I had no family," he said. "I had less to lose. I would help them against Pan. But . . . "

Pepper folded his arms. "It's already seen you. You're already dead."

That sunk in. Stanuel had handled emergencies. Breaches, where vacuum flooded in, sucking the air out. He'd survived explosions, dumb mistakes, and even being speared by a piece of rebar. All by keeping cool and doing what needed to be done.

He hadn't expected, when told that he'd need to let in an assassin, that he'd become this involved. But what did he expect? That he could be part of the resistance and not ever risk his life? He'd risked it the moment one of his co-workers had started whispering to him, talking about overthrowing Pan, and he'd only stood there and listened.

resistance

Stanuel took a deep breath and nodded. "Okay. I'm sorry."

The space station Haven was a classic wheel, rotating slowly to provide some degree of gravity for its inhabitants so that they did not have to lose bone mass and muscle, the price of living in no gravity.

At Haven's center lay the hub. Here lay an atrium, the extraordinary no-gravity gardens and play areas for Haven's citizens. Auditoriums and pools and labs and tourist areas and fields, the heart of the community. Dripping down from the hub, docking ports, airlocks, antennae, and spare mass from the original asteroid Haven had taken its metals. This was where they floated now.

But on the other side of the hub hung a long and spindly structure that had once housed the central command for the station. A bridge, of sorts, with a view of all of Haven, sat at the very tip of the tower. The bridge was duplicated just below in the form of an observation deck and restaurant for visitors and proud citizens and school trips.

All things the tower existed for in that more innocent time *before*.

Now Pan sat in the bridge, looking out at all of them, both through the large portal-like windows up there, and through the network of rovers and insect cams scattered throughout Haven.

One of which Pepper had just flattened.

Stanuel knew they no longer had an hour now.

• • •

seeds of change

PEPPER SQUATTED IN front of the hatch. "It's good I'm not claustrophobic."

"This runs all the way to the restaurant at the tower. It's the fastest way there."

"If we don't choke on fumes and grease first." Pepper scraped grease off the inside.

Stanuel handed him a mask with filters from the tiny utility closet underneath the pipe. He also found a set of headlamps. "Get in, I'll follow, we need to hurry."

Pepper hauled himself into the tube and Stanuel followed, worming his way in. When he closed the hatch after them the darkness seemed infinite until Pepper clicked a tiny penlight on.

Moving down the tube was simple enough. They were in the hub. They were weightless. They could use their fingertips to slowly move their way along.

After several minutes Pepper asked, voice muffled by the filter, "So how did it happen? Haven was one of the most committed to the idea of techno-democracy."

There were hundreds of little bubbles of life scattered all throughout the asteroid belt, hidden away from the mess of Earth and her orbit by distance and anonymity. Each one a petri dish of politics and culture. Each a pearl formed around a bit of asteroid dirt that birthed it.

"There are problems with a techno-democracy," muttered Stanuel. "If you're a purist, like we were, you had to have the citizenry decide on everything." The sheer

resistance

amount of things that a society needed decided had almost crushed them.

Every minute everyone had to decide something. Pass a new law. Agree to send delegates to another station. Accept taxes. Divvy out taxes. Pay a bill. The stream of decisions became overwhelming, constantly popping up and requiring an electronic yes or no. And research was needed for each decision.

"The artificial intelligence modelers came up with our solution. They created intelligences that would vote just as you would if you had the time to do nothing but focus on voting." They weren't real artificial intelligences. The modelers took your voting record, and paired it to your buying habits, social habits, and all the other aspects of your life that were tracked in modern life to model your habits. After all, if a bank could use a financial profile to figure out if an unusual purchase didn't reflect the buyer's habits and freeze an account for safety reasons, why couldn't the same black box logic be applied to a voter's patterns?

Pepper snorted. "You turned over your voting to machines."

Stanuel shook his head, making the headlamp's light dart from side to side. "Not machines. *Us*. The profiles were incredible. They modeled what votes were important enough—or that the profilers were uncertain to get right—so that they only passed on the important ones to us. They were like spam filters for voting. They freed us from the

seeds of change

incredible flood of meaningless minutiae that the daily running of a government needed."

"But they failed," Pepper grunted.

"Yes and no . . ."

"Quiet." Pepper pointed his penlight down. "I hear something. Clinking around back the way we came from."

"Someone chasing us?"

"No. It's mechanical."

Stanuel thought about it for a moment. He couldn't think of anything. "Rover?"

Pepper stopped and Stanuel collided with his boots. "So our time has run out."

"I don't know."

A faint clang echoed around them. "Back up," Pepper said, pushing him away with a quick shove of the boot to the top of his head.

"What are you doing?"

"We've come far enough." Four extremely loud bangs filled the tube with absurdly bright flashes of light. Pepper moved out through the ragged rip in the pipe.

Another large wall blocked him. "What is this?"

Stanuel, still blinking, looked at it from still inside the pipe. "You'll want the other side. Nothing but vacuum on the other side." Had Pepper used more explosive they might have just been blown right out the side of Haven.

"Right." Pepper twisted further out, and another explosion rocked the pipe.

resistance

When Stanuel wriggled out and around the tube he saw trees. They'd blown a hole in the lawn of the gardens. They carefully climbed out, pushing past dirt, and the tubes and support equipment that monitored and maintained the gardens and soaked the roots with water.

"Now what?" Stanuel asked. "We're going to be seen."

"Now it gets messy," Pepper said. He pulled Stanuel along toward the large elevator at the center. "I'm going with a frontal assault. It'll be messy. But . . . I do well at messy."

"There's no reason for me to be here, then," Stanuel said. "What use will I be? I failed to get you there through the exhaust pipes. Why not just let me go?"

Pepper laughed. "Not quite ready to die for the cause, Stanuel?"

"No. Yes. I'm not sure, it just feels like suicide, and I'm not sure who that helps."

"You're safer with me." Pepper launched them from branch to branch through the trees. Now that curfews were in effect, no families perched in the great globe of green, no kids screaming and racing through the trees. It was eerily silent.

Pepper slowed them down in the last grove of trees before the elevators at the core of the gardens. As they gently floated towards the lobby at the bottom of the shaft three well-built men, the kind who obviously trained their bodies up on the rim of the wheel, turned the corner.

They carried stun guns. Non-lethal, but still menacing.

seeds of change

Stanuel heard a click. Pepper held out a gun in each hand. Real guns, perfectly lethal.

"I'd turn those off," Pepper said to the men, "and pass them over, and then no one would get hurt."

They hesitated. But then the commanding voice of Pan filled the gardens. "Do as he says. And then escort him to me."

They looked at each other, unhappy, and tossed the guns over. Pepper threw them off into the trees. "You're escorting us?"

The three unhappy security men nodded. "Pan says you have an electro-magnetic pulse weapon. We're not to provoke you."

Stanuel bit his lip. It felt like a trap. These traitors were taking them into the maw of the beast, and Pepper, as far as he could see, looked cheerful about it. "It's a trap," he muttered.

"Well, of course it is," Pepper said. "But it's a good one that avoids us skulking about, getting dirtier, or having to shoot our way through." The mercenary followed Pan's lackeys into the elevator. He turned and looked at Stanuel, hovering outside. "And Pan's right. I do have an E.M.P device. But if I trigger it this deep into the hub, I take out all your power generating capabilities and computer core systems."

"Really?" Stanuel was intrigued.

Pepper held up a tiny metal tube with a button on the end. "If I get to the tower," Pepper said. "I can trigger it

resistance

and take out Pan, while leaving the rest of the station unaffected."

Stanuel had weathered five days of his beloved Haven under the autocratic rule of Pan, the trickster.

He'd travel with Pepper to see it end, he realized.

He pulled himself into the elevator.

FOR FIVE DAYS Haven's populace had a ruler, a single being whose word was law, whose thoughts were made policy. Pan stood in the center of the command console, its face lit by the light of a hundred screens and the reflections off the inner rim of Haven's great wheel.

Pan wore a simple blue suit, had tan skin, brown eyes, and brown hair. His androgynous face and thin body meant that had he stood in a crowd of Haven's citizens, he would hardly have been noticed. He could be anybody, or everybody.

He also flickered slightly as he turned.

"My executioner and his companion. I'm delighted," Pan said. "If I could shake your hand, I would." He gave a slight bow.

Pepper returned it.

Pan smiled. "I've been waiting for you two for quite a while. I apologize for sending the rover up the exhaust pipe."

Pepper shrugged. "No matter. So what now? I have something that can take you out, you have me surrounded by nasty surprises . . ."

seeds of change

Pan folded its arms. "I don't do nasty surprises, Pepper. I'm not a monster, contrary to what Stanuel might say. You have an E.M.P device, and if you were to set it off further down the tower, you would shut all Haven down. True, I have backup capabilities that mitigate that, but your device presents a terrible risk to the well being of the citizenry. With the device and you up here, the only risk is to me."

An easy enough decision, Stanuel thought. Trigger the damn device! But Pepper glanced around the room, maybe seeing traps that Stanuel couldn't. "If you don't do nasty surprises, what stops me from zapping you out, right here, right now?"

"I would like to make you an offer. If you'd listen."

Pepper's lips quirked. "I wouldn't be much of a mercenary if I just accepted the higher bid in the middle of the job. You don't get repeat work very often that way."

Pan held its hands up. "I understand. But consider this, I am, indirectly, the one who hired you."

Stanuel had to object. "The resistance..."

"I run it," Pan smiled. "I know everything it does, who it hires, and in many cases, I give it the orders."

Stanuel felt like he'd been thrown into a freezing cold vat of water. He lost his breath. "What do you mean? You infiltrated it?" They had lost, even before they'd started.

Pan turned to the mercenary. "Stanuel is bewildered, as are many, by what they created, Pepper. I'm merely the amalgamated avatar of the converged will of all the simulations made to run this colony. The voter simulations kept

resistance

taking up energy, so the master processing program came up with a more elegant solution: me. Why run millions of emulators, when it could fuse them all into a single expression of its will that would run the government?"

"A clever solution," Pepper said.

"A techno-democracy, even more so than the vanilla kind, is messy. Dangerously so. With study committees and votes on everything, things that needed to be done quickly didn't get done in time.

"So the emulations decided to put forward a bill, buried in the middle of some other obscure administrivia. The vote was that emulations be given command of the government."

Stanuel stepped forward. "We woke up and found that in a single moment all of Haven had been disenfranchised."

"By your own desires and predictive voting algorithms," Pan said. "In a way, yes. In a way, no."

Stanuel spit at the dictatorial hologram in front him. "Then the emulators decided that a single amalgamation, an avatar, and expression of all their wills, would work better. So then even our own voting patterns turned over their power."

"Not surprising," Pepper said. "You didn't have the maturity to keep your own vote, you turned it over to the copies of yourselves. Why be surprised that the copies would do something similar and turn to a benevolent dictator of their own creation?"

seeds of change

Pan looked pleased. "Dictators aren't so bad, if they're the right dictator. And it's hard coded into my very being to look out for the community. That's why I look like this." It waved a hand over its face. "I'm the average of all the faces in Haven. Political poll modeling shows that were I to run for office, it would be almost guaranteed based on physiological responses alone."

Stanuel looked at Pepper. "Pan may have infiltrated, but you were still paid to destroy it. Do it."

"No," Pan said. "You might pull that trigger. But if you do, you destroy what the people of Haven really wanted, what they desired, and what they worked very hard to create, Pepper, even if they didn't realize they consciously wanted it."

"I've heard you get the government you deserve," Pepper said. "But this is something else. They created their own tyranny..."

"But, Pepper, I'm not a tyrant. If they vote as a whole to oust me, they can do it."

Pepper moved over to the one of great windows to look out at the inside rim of Haven. Thousands of distant portholes dotted the giant wheel, lit up by the people living inside the rooms across from them.

"Look around you," Pan implored. "There are plenty who like what I'm doing. I'm rebuilding parts of Haven that have been neglected for years. I'm improving agriculture as we speak. I've made the choices that were hard, got things into motion that just sat there while people

resistance

quibbled over them. I am *action*. I am *progress*."

Stanuel kicked forward and Pepper glanced back at him. "I think Stanuel objects."

Pan sighed. "Yes, a few will be disaffected. They will always be disaffected. That was why I created outlets for the disaffected, because they are a part of me as well. But my plea to you, Pepper, is not to break this great experiment. I can offer you more money, a place of safety here whenever you would want it, and Haven as a powerful ally to your needs."

Pepper nodded and sat in the air, his legs folded. "I have a question."

"Proceed."

"Why do they call you Pan?"

"They call me Pan because it's short for panopticon. An old experiment: if you were to create a round jail with a tower in the center, with open cell walls facing it, and the ability to look into every cell, you would have the ultimate surveillance society. The panopticon. In some ways, Haven is just that, with me at its center."

Pepper chuckled. "I'd half expected some insane military dictator wearing a head of antlers calling himself Pan."

Pan did not laugh. It leaned closer. "Pepper, understand me. This is not your fight. I'm the naturally elected ruler of Haven. The *choice* to remove me, that isn't yours. I did not bring you here to destroy me, but for other reasons."

seeds of change

"The choice?" The word affected Pepper in some way Stanuel could not figure out. He looked over at Stanuel. "Then if you're a benevolent ruler, you will escort me off Haven, leave Stanuel alive, and move on to other things. After all, it was your orders that set Stanuel down this path."

"Of course. It's that or a sentence in one of Haven's residential rooms. You'll be locked in, but comfortable. There do have to be ways to handle such things. Exile, or confinement."

"Okay, Mr. Pan. Okay. My work here is done." Pepper moved towards Stanuel with a flick of his feet. "Come on Stanuel, it's time to leave the tower."

STANUEL COULD HARDLY look Pepper in the eye. "I can't believe you left there."

"Pan made a good argument."

"Pan offered to pay you more. That's all."

"There's that, but I won't take it." Pepper scratched his head. "If I destroyed Pan, what would you do?"

Stanuel frowned. "What do you mean?"

"You said the emulations wouldn't be allowed to hold direct control, earlier. Does that mean you'd allow the emulations to come back and decide votes for you?"

"One assumes. We might have not gotten them right, but if we can fix that error, things can go back to the way they were."

Pepper unpacked his suit and stepped into it. It crin-

resistance

kled and cracked as he zipped it up. "And then I'll be back. Because you'll repeat the same pattern all over again."

"What?"

"For all your assumptions, you're not quite seeing the pattern. Deep down, somewhere, you all want Pan. You don't want the responsibility of voting, you want the easy result."

"That's not true," Stanuel objected.

"Oh come on. Think of all the times princes and princesses are adored and feted. Think of all the actors and great people we adore and fawn over."

"That doesn't make us slavish followers."

Pepper cocked his head. "No, but we still can't escape the instincts we carry from being a small band of hunter-gatherers making their way across a plain, depending on a single leader who knew the ins and outs of their tiny tribe and listened to their feedback. That doesn't scale, so we have inelegant hacks around it.

"Stanuel, you all created a technological creature, able to view you all and listen to all your feedback, and embody a benevolent single tribal leader. Not only was it born out of your unconscious needs, even your own emulations overwhelmingly voted it into power as sole ruler of Haven."

Stanuel raised his hand to halt Pepper. "That's all true, and over the last four days we've argued around all this when we found out about the vote. But, Pepper, whether perfect or not, we can't allow a single person to rule us. It goes against everything we believe in, everything we worked for when we created Haven."

Pepper nodded. "I know."

"And you're going to walk away."

"I have to. Because this wasn't some power grab, it was the will of your people. There was a vote. Pan is right, it *is* the rightful ruler. But," Pepper pointed at him, "I'm not leaving you empty-handed."

"What do you mean?"

He handed over the backpack and pressed a small stick with a button into Stanuel's hand. "The E.M.P device is in the backpack. You won't get anywhere near the tower to take out just Pan, but if you trigged it in the hub after I leave, it will shut Haven down. Pan will have backups, and his supporters will protect the tower, but if enough people feel like you do, you can storm it with the guns in that pack."

"You're asking me to . . . fight?"

"You know your history. The tree of liberty needs to be watered with some blood every now and then. Thomas Jefferson, I think, said that. Most of your ancestors fought for it. You could have kept it, had you just taken the time to vote yourself instead of leaving it to something else."

"I don't know if I can." Stanuel was bewildered. He'd never done anything violent in his life.

Pepper smiled. "You might find Pan is more willing to fold than you imagine. Think about it."

With that, he stepped into the airlock. The door shut with a hiss, and the spacesuit faded into camouflage black

resistance

as Pepper disappeared inside whatever stealth ship had bought him to Haven.

Stanuel stood there. He pulled the backpack's straps up over onto his shoulders and made his way toward the gardens, mulling over the mercenary's last words.

A hologram of Pan waited for him at the entrance to the gardens, but no goons were nearby. Stanuel had expected to be captured, with the threat of a long confinement ahead of him. But it was just the electronic god of Haven and Stanuel.

"You didn't understand what he meant, did you?" Pan said. It really was the panopticon, listening to everything that happened in Haven.

"No." Stanuel held the switch to the E.M.P in his hand, waiting for some trick. Was he going to get shot in the head by a sniper? But Pan said it didn't use violence.

Maybe a tranquilizer dart of some sort?

"I told you," Pan said, "I also created the resistance."

"But that doesn't make any sense," Stanuel said.

"It does if you stop thinking of me as a person, but as an avatar of your collective emulators. Every ruling system has an opposition; the day after I was voted into power, I had to create a series of checks and balances against myself. That was the resistance."

"But I was recruited by people."

"And they were recruited by my people, working for me, who were told they were to create an opposition tame as a honey trap." Pan flickered as he walked through a tree.

seeds of change

An incongruous vision, as Stanuel floated through the no gravity garden.

"Why would you want to die?"

"Because, I may not be what all of you want, just what *most* of you want. I have to create an opportunity for myself to be stopped, or else, I really am a tyrant and not the best solution. That is why Pepper was hired to bring the E.M.P device aboard. That was why, ultimately, he left it with you."

"So it's all in my hands," Stanuel said.

"Yes. Live in a better economy, a safer economy, but one ruled by what you have created. Or muddle along yourselves." Pan moved in front of Stanuel, floating with him.

Stanuel held up the metal tube and hovered his thumb over the button. "Men should be free."

Pan nodded sadly. "But Stanuel, you all will never be able to get things done the way I can. It will be such a mess of compromise, personality, mistakes, wrong choices, emotional choices, mob rule, and imperfect decisions. You could well destroy Haven with your imprecise decisions."

It was a siren call. But even though Pan was perfect, and right, it was the same song that led smart men to call tyrants leaders and do so happily. The promise of quick action, clean and fast decisions.

Alluring.

"I know it will be messy," Stanuel said, voice quavering. "And I have no idea how it will work out. But at least it will be *ours*."

resistance

He pressed the button and watched as the lights throughout Haven dimmed and flickered. Pan disappeared with a sigh, a ghost banished. The darkness marched its glorious way through the cavernous gardens toward Stanuel, who folded up in the air by a tree while he waited for the dark to take him in its freeing embrace.